Contents

THE TREE WITH EYES

Bela Negi is a filmmaker and writer based between Mumbai and Nainital. A graduate of the Film and Television Institute of India, Pune, she has worked in cinema for over two decades, writing, directing and editing across formats. Her debut feature, *Daayen Ya Baayen* (2010), set in a Himalayan village, reflects her long engagement with the social and environmental realities of the region. It was one of the first works to carve a space for the lives and people of Uttarakhand on the silver screen.

She is the co-founder of Nitric Films—a film production house—and the founder of the Leafbird Foundation, which works in remote Himalayan communities on education, environmental conservation and sustainable livelihoods.

The Tree with Eyes marks her first collection of short fiction. She continues to work across film and literature while engaging with younger practitioners through teaching and workshops.

BELA NEGI

THE TREE WITH EYES

AND OTHER STORIES

First published by Tranquebar, an imprint of Westland Books, a division of Nasadiya Technologies Private Limited, in 2026

No. 269/2B, First Floor, 'Irai Arul', Vimalraj Street, Nethaji Nagar, Alapakkam Main Road, Maduravoyal, Chennai 600095

Westland, the Westland logo, Tranquebar and the Tranquebar logo are the trademarks of Nasadiya Technologies Private Limited, or its affiliates.

'The Way Home' was first published in *Kitaab*'s Best Asian Short Stories 2021; 'Gangrene' was published in *Out of Print*; 'The Tree with Eyes' was published in *Gulmohar Quarterly*.

ISBN: 9789371976824

10 9 8 7 6 5 4 3 2 1

Typeset by Jojy Philip

Printed at Parksons Graphics Pvt. Ltd

Dedicated to the countless voices of our mountains
whose stories may never reach the page,
yet are the life they breathe

And to my parents and my aunts
who could find moments of laughter
in even the saddest tale

The Tree with Eyes

Lata's breathing quickened as she ground into the lumpy cotton pillow in an attempt to pleasure herself. Tucked under a thick blanket, she made as little movement as possible even though she was alone in the room. In the quiet of the night the wooden floorboards amplified even the slightest shuffle. She thought of her husband, but the memory of his clumsy and indifferent touch dispelled her ardour instantly. Throwing away the covers, she flipped onto her back and looked at the high ceiling that had blackened over time with the soot from the kitchen fire. She ran her restless eyes along the length of the bulky logs that formed a wooden framework for the stone-tiled roof. If one were to hang oneself from one of the wooden beams, she thought, it would hold up very well. Or if the house were set on fire, it was fortified with so much wood, it would blaze to the ground in no time. She chided herself for having such a thought at all, but the image lingered, dry and brittle, like ash that refused to settle.

She still felt overwhelmed by the rich, subtle aroma of rosewood furniture brought up with effort from the plains. She inhaled deeply, trying to recall the sharper smell of cheap unpolished pinewood of the low ceilings in her parents' house, a smell intertwined with the constant yearning she felt for that home she had left behind.

She sat up in bed and looked at her reflection in the mirror of the heavy oak cabinet. Only her large doe-like eyes were visible in the darkness. She touched her soft cheek and ran her hands down the curves of her body. Suddenly feeling suffocated with the unquenched fire in her groin and thoughts of blazing flames in her head, she threw open the window, letting the night air rush in.

Resting her chin on the windowpane, she closed her eyes and took a deep sip of the cool air. The knot of despair, that had sat tight in her stomach for several days, refused to loosen. She thought again of her husband, who had left a month ago for his army posting at the border, to a non-family station. He had gone away a couple of weeks after their marriage and would hold that posting for at least another year.

Opening her eyes, she looked at the jacaranda tree standing in the gently sloping landscape in the fields beyond, its pale flowers gleaming in the moonlight. Surrounded by darkness, the tree stood absolutely still as if it was hiding several mysteries in its fold. It was at that point that she heard the grunts. At first she was alarmed. Was it a panther on the prowl? But what followed were soft moans. She cringed instinctively, realising that it was her in-laws making love in the room downstairs. She listened for a while, and when there was no doubt about the source of the sounds, she closed the window stealthily, as if afraid of being caught in the act of eavesdropping. Slipping back into bed, she covered her face again in a bid to block those sounds from her head.

She was accustomed to getting up at the crack of dawn. Even as a young girl she had had to finish several chores before heading to school. But that day, embarrassed about the previous night's unintentional eavesdropping, she was reluctant to face her in-laws and lay in bed till she heard them finish their morning tea and open the front door. She was relieved when, through the crack in the window, she saw her father-in-law walking down the slope towards the motorable road with a rifle on his shoulder.

When she went into the kitchen her mother-in-law had taken her seat for the day next to the main choolah. In her late forties, Savitri had a clear complexion and strong features. As Lata stole a look at her stoic face, she imagined her in the throes of passion. The thought was amusing and uncomfortable at the same time. Savitri handed Lata a glass of tea while looking out of the window. Lata had noticed that she never looked directly at her, instead always gazing in her general direction. Initially, Lata thought it was because Savitri was a reserved person. But it didn't take her long to understand that it was because she had no real interest in her, as if Lata as an individual did not matter to her. Despite her being in the house for almost two months, there was hardly any conversation between them except of a functional nature—the clothes that needed to be washed, the cow's foot that needed medication, or the rice that needed to be threshed. Whenever Lata tried talking to her about her life before marriage, she would turn away and busy herself. But while reticent, Savitri had a way of being domineering, and Lata had learnt to live by her rules.

Pouring some tea for herself, Savitri informed her that her father-in-law had gone to the neighbouring village for a few days. Leopard attacks on humans had increased in the recent years, and Hukum Singh often assisted the forest department in hunting down these man-eaters. For this purpose, he kept a licensed rifle at home, inspiring awe in the villagers. As a wood contractor, he spent a lot of time in the forest and hunted gamebirds and other small and large prey. If there ever had been any fear of the villagers complaining to forest officials, Hukum had handled it by gifting them small game now and then. Lata had to learn to skin, clean and chop the game which he brought home.

After herding the cows to graze in the pasture for the day, Lata didn't head back immediately. She went into the shaded alcove of the flourishing jacaranda tree, which was nurturing a profusion of life under its spread. She sat on a rotting tree trunk that was surrounded by a mauve carpet of fallen jacaranda flowers. Above, the branches of the tree formed a pretty mesh against the blue sky. She had not seen these trees in the higher mountains where she came from, and these summer blooms delighted her. The trees were usually found along hill roads, she had noticed, but this particular seed had wandered far from the road, found its way into these fields and finding an available plot had built a home.

The last time she sat here, village women, on their way to the forest to cut wood, had told her in hushed tones about Malti Amma, long dead and gone, who, having indulged in an indiscretion in her youth, had buried her illegitimate child under this very tree as soon as it was born and still alive. Perhaps that particular uncharacteristically twisted branch of the tree had been nourished by the baby's flesh, Lata thought with macabre fascination as she looked up at the canopy against the sky. Then getting up reluctantly she headed back to the sacks of rice that were waiting to be threshed.

Before her marriage Lata's friends had envied her. They imagined her following her husband from from one posting to another, living a lighter life than the one they knew awaited them. No girl willingly stayed back in the village after marriage; it meant a future measured in heat, dust, and labour that crept into the bones and wore their beauty down early. Lata too had been hopeful, planning her new life away from the toils of daily life. When she thought about it now, she wondered if this arrangement of her having to stay back in the village had been explained to her family before marriage. The match had appeared too good to question closely.

Hukum Singh was the largest wood contractor in the region, a man whose prosperity was spoken of with a mix of respect and caution. Of his two children, his daughter lived comfortably in Delhi, while his son, Aalam, was a jawaan in the army. Though Aalam was the unquestioned heir to the business, Hukum believed the army would temper and harden him before he returned to take charge of what was already his.

Lata's parents, aware of her delicate beauty, had quietly hoped for a match that exceeded what their circumstances would normally permit. They were, therefore, both surprised and gratified when Hukum Singh proposed his son. The arrangement was brokered through one of Lata's cousins who worked under him. In the neighbourhood, envy took the form of whispers: that a poor bride had been chosen deliberately for Aalam, one whose expectations would be modest and whose obedience could be taken for granted.

When Hukum Singh and his wife Savitri Devi arrived for the first round of talks, Lata was in the backyard with Chandan, trying to console him. Chandan had been one of the few boys from the village to make it as far as Nainital, a posh hill station in the region, for university. Sending a son so far was rare, and it meant that Chandan's parents had faith in a future beyond farming for him. When he returned for the first time, his newly gained swagger gave him the confidence to declare his undying love for Lata. Her beauty had always needed a suitable admirer and a town-returned Chandan's attentions felt like a reaffirmation of the moniker the local boys had given her—'Aishwarya Rai of Block Kapkot'.

They sealed their young romance with kisses stolen deep inside the forest, in patches of dappled light beneath tall deodar trees. In that hushed pocket of the world, where only the treetops whispered to one another, those kisses felt enough. They promised a life of unending ardour and fulfilment. They decided to wait before speaking to their parents, agreeing it would be wiser once Chandan had finished college and secured some kind of employment. Lata was certain of one thing: she did not want a life bound to the village. She longed to see the world.

In the backyard now she promised Chandan that she would not yield to pressure or temptation, no matter how wealthy or powerful the proposal might be. Reassured by her resolve, Chandan left, believing their future was intact.

As she served tea to Hukum and Savitri, however, her heart quietly sank. They were a dignified and handsome couple, unlike anyone she had known before and certainly unlike those in her own home. To refuse such people would feel outrageous to her parents and crush their hopes.

When Hukum added that they sought no dowry, a chill ran through her. The last foothold for refusal vanished. With three younger sisters behind her, she knew too well the strain her parents lived under and how worry governed every decision they made for the future.

After a sleepless night, she told her parents, who valued her opinions, that she was willing to meet the prospective groom. The meeting never took place. Hukum dismissed such encounters as a modern indulgence but promised instead to send a photograph of Aalam at the earliest.

Though jilting Chandan lay heavily on Lata, she could not ignore the transformation the proposal had brought about at home. Her father walked about smiling foolishly to himself, while her mother spoke openly of the beautiful grandchildren she would one day have. For several nights, Lata cried into her pillow, soaking it with quiet cold tears, her stifled cries battling the remorse that she felt so keenly.

But soon, with the arrival of Aalam's photograph, tall and dashing in his army uniform, the thought of Chandan, hanging around the village marketplace in his shiny shoes and bright clothes, began to arouse pity in Lata. And pity was no recipe to battle the rising ardour she began to feel for Aalam. As the wedding had to take place within a fortnight, before Aalam's leave from duty expired, Lata did not have much time to indulge in guilt for breaking Chandan's heart. But it would linger, and later, on those lonely autumn afternoons, it would come back to create a storm in her life.

A few days before the wedding it transpired that while Hukum Singh, a man of few words, had not made any specific dowry demand, he conveyed the message that 'what was appropriate should be given' and that the wedding arrangements 'should be in keeping with our standing in society'. Lata's father agonised about what would be appropriate and took a small loan from his neighbours to do the best he could. He gave his wife a small amount to put together some bridal finery for Lata, which she did hurriedly, allowing Lata to choose the best fabrics available in the village. He remained on edge throughout the wedding, his gentle face drawn tight with anxiety. Lata felt a stab of pain watching his slight frame stand so obsequiously beside the solid, imposing Hukum. Her own family seemed made of a softer, smaller grain compared to her husband's family. When the groom's family offered no comment on the dowry or arrangements, her father took their silence as approval.

Little girls, awed by Lata's delicate beauty, flocked around her, giggling continuously and tugging at her ghaghra during the bidai. While Lata sobbed helplessly, bidding her parents farewell, her father looked immensely relieved as he bundled her off into a decorated jeep.

Sitting next to Aalam, she looked out of the moving jeep at the receding vista of her village, an immense sadness wrenching her heart. Those forests where she had spent so much of her childhood gathering wood and picking berries … she could smell the fresh stillness of mornings shared with Chandan. … Was that him standing high up on the hillside, that flash of an orange shirt? Before she could take a closer look, the jeep took a sharp turn, and the hillside was not visible anymore. Soon motion sickness displaced her sorrow, and after retching by the roadside, she fell into an exhausted sleep. The jeep moved down the winding road, a small dot on the back of the white serpentine road that uncoiled endlessly and soon disappeared into the folds of the mountains.

When she woke up, they were moving past warm pine forests. The roads had more traffic, which whizzed past with a blast of film music. Her mood had lightened. She stole a look at Aalam, asleep beside her, the firmness of his jaw softened by rest, and smiled.

Aalam's village was on a gentle hillslope on the bank of the same river that rushed down the steep mountains past Lata's village and settled into a languid flow in this flat open valley. The land was moist and fertile, the fields lay fuller, more abundant than those she had known.

She was surprised and disappointed to see that her new home, though a confident portrayal of an affluent household and far larger than other village houses, was not modernised at all. Built of stone and slate, it lacked the colourful flourishes that cement houses allowed. Inside, the rooms were heavily fortified with wood, the walls still coated with mud. The carved doors and windows, dignified in their bare simplicity, left her unmoved. Coming into money a little late in life, Hukum insisted on living simply, with only a fridge, TV and motorcycle to count for as urban comforts. A motorable road did not come right up to the house and one had to walk about half a kilometre on foot to get to it. But the house was distinctive, separated from other village homes by a large fruit orchard and broad terraced fields where they grew wheat and rice.

That night Aalam did not speak to Lata at all. He hurriedly turned off the lights before clumsily groping at her in the dark and after thrusting into her a few times, rolled off and fell into a deep slumber. Lata lay there feeling empty. In the next few days, she made awkward attempts at having conversations with him but he just proved to be dull and unresponsive. She soon noticed how he cowered in his father's presence and how fiercely his mother Savitri shielded him. Hukum Singh had an imposing air about him. Even Lata found herself instinctively shrinking into silence when he was around. He never raised his deep measured voice but his eyes, under the heavy full brow, were sharp and piercing. Often when Hukum appeared to be speaking to Aalam in that unhurried drawl, Lata realised he was berating him, while Savitri, also speaking in her normal tone, was defending him fiercely. Somehow she found this to be more disturbing than a loud altercation would have been. Seeing her young husband reduced to a quivering child by a mere taunt was very disturbing for her, and it made her think of him with more tenderness.

A few days later, she heard Hukum taunting Aalam more openly, mocking him for complaining about having to return to duty. When Lata realised that she was not to accompany him and that it would be a year before his return, she couldn't contain her emotions. She stormed off into her room, throwing urgent looks over her shoulder for Aalam to follow. She had to wait for a long time before he appeared. She clung onto him and cried bitterly. He kept repeating that he did not want to go back himself, that he hated his job, but he refused to acknowledge, even for a moment, her hurt and disappointment. Lata threatened in harsh whispers to return to her maika. The next day, as if anticipating her defiance, Hukum bought her a set of gold ornaments from the biggest jeweller in the nearby town. It was a heavy gold choker in a traditional design with two matching gold earrings. Even though Lata would have preferred a lighter piece in a modern design, she recognised its worth and was flattered to have been wooed into compliance. Savitri, who rarely betrayed any emotion otherwise, looked distinctly displeased and refused to acknowledge Lata's presence for a few days.

On the night before he was to leave, Lata found Aalam sitting in their room, withdrawn and silent. She closed the door, sat beside him on the bed and wrapped her arms around his neck. She leaned in, offering him what she had been holding back all day, her mouth searching gently for his. His response came abruptly. He pulled her towards him, turned off the light, and stripped her of her clothes with hurried hands. In the darkness, Lata yielded, her body answering while her heart slowly retreated. What she had meant to give him, the tenderness, the warmth, stayed with her, untouched.

With Aalam gone, Lata found herself immersed in a routine which was not very different from the one in her parental home. Cooking and all the chores of the kitchen were Savitri's domain while the rest of the household work fell to Lata. There was no help except for harvesting the crop. Aalam's sister had taken care of the household chores till her marriage a few months ago. Suddenly it all made sense to Lata, the urgency in getting Aalam married during his short leave, the ostensible lack of a demand for dowry, the subtle pressure. The help that was hired in the interim period was relieved soon after the wedding. It was difficult to tell whether the family's insistence on a simple way of living was a matter of frugality or a kind of stern humility.

Savitri wore, for everyday use, just two saris, both worn thin with time, alternating between them. Even Hukum remained in old, faded clothes at home, changing into more respectable ones only when he went out for work. The bright, new clothes Lata had had tailored felt out of place within the house. However, she hesitated to ask for simpler ones so soon, unsure of how to make her needs known.

Soon, with so little communication of any kind, Lata's effervescence began to wither away. She sought to interact with the village women, but the house was slightly cut off from the village, and more than that, Savitri clearly disapproved. Wary of that uneasy silence which seemed to settle over the house, Lata would retreat to her own room as soon as her work was finished.

Because of Aalam's remote posting the family could not call him. Lata waited for his weekly calls but he always called on his father' phone, asking to speak to her only after he had spoken to his parents. Their conversations were brief and guarded, with Hukum never far away. With her own family she spoke every other day, careful to keep her voice light, betraying no hint of the disappointment she was learning to live with.

Hukum returned earlier than expected from the hunt for the man-eating leopard. He had killed two jungle fowls too and handed them to Lata for skinning. Savitri disliked the task. As they ate in the dimly lit kitchen, he spoke of the leopard, mentioning casually that his last kill had been a young boy out in the jungle with his goats. The boy's body, he said, had been used as bait, with a trap set close by. It had been an easy kill. Someone from the forest department had shot the leopard the moment it was caught.

As he said this, Lata saw Hukum's body stiffen, a brief, unmistakable tension, as though he had been robbed of the pleasure of firing the fatal shot himself. Savitri, however, who had been tightly wound up since his departure, seemed to loosen at the news, her breath coming easier.

Lata remembered what she had heard from the village woman on their way to the forest. The previous year, Hukum had injured and trapped another man-eating leopard in a cave in a neighbouring jungle. He had not killed it at once. Instead, he had camped nearby, keeping watch as the wounded animal growled in rage and fear, growing weaker each day from its bleeding wounds. Only when the forest department got wind of it they intervened, forcing him to put the animal down.

Now, as Lata watched Hukum eat, his clean-cut face gave nothing away. There was no sign of that brutality in his countenance. But it was his eyes. She had seen that same flicker in them when he ruthlessly belittled Aalam, and could imagine that they glinted with the same fire when he tortured the leopard.

When Aalam called that night, Lata retreated into a corner and spoke in whispers, asking him to promise that he would not leave his job. He was quiet for a moment and then asked about the rice harvest. Later, when she opened her window for fresh air, she heard them again. Hukum's coarse grunts followed by Savitri's muted moans. Somehow, she felt more disturbed by them that day than she had the first time.

The next day there was a photograph in the newspaper. Hukum stood with the forest officials beside a dead leopard tied to a stake. He sat in the sunlit courtyard studying the picture while Lata threshed rice nearby, sweat gathering at her temples in the late morning heat. Savitri came out carrying a katori of mustard oil and began to massage Hukum's bare torso.

Lata stole a look at them, noticing his muscled arms, his still lean body, and images of him writhing over Savitri, of him thrusting into her kept coming to her mind. She startled when she realised he had caught her looking at him as she bent to serve him hot coals for his hukka. She hurried away guiltily, afraid he had read her thoughts. She had become aware of his agile gait, that of a skilled hunter, which gave him such a light tread that you would often not hear him enter the room till you saw him. His presence filled the house in ways that unsettled her, even though she hardly had any interaction with him. Sometimes she felt his watchful gaze as she went about her chores with a vigour that belied her delicate frame.

Unused to the heat in these lower climes, she needed to take a short rest in the afternoon as summer set in. From her window she watched the village women on the opposite hill, their voices carrying as they laughed and called out to one another while working in the fields. On this side, the land lay quiet, golden with the ripe wheat crop. This landscape that had seemed so luscious when she first came now seemed desolate. The high sun made everything look parched and jaundiced.

As evening approached, sounds from across the hill died down. The deepening shadows gathered in uneven patches, stirring in her a vague but persistent despair. She told herself that it was only for a year. Then she would leave to be with her husband. Yet somewhere beneath that reasoning lay a suspicion she did not want to examine too closely. Aalam's voice on the phone had already begun to sound unfamiliar, as though it belonged to someone she no longer knew.

She stood before the mirror, slowly combing out her long brown hair. There was only herself to take pleasure in her beauty.

After her short rest she would step out into the stone courtyard which burned bright in the high sun. Against it her slim silhouette could be seen working unflaggingly till evening, threshing, pounding, cleaning, washing, flogging out all unnecessary thoughts from her head. As dusk gathered, she would go into the forest and call in the cows.

Savitri refused to let Lata visit her parental home as was customary a couple of months after marriage. Instead, her father and youngest sister visited her. Lata had been waiting for them eagerly, longing, for a few days at least, to feel like her old self again. But when they arrived, she was immediately stung by their restraint, by the deep awkwardness they carried with them into the house.

Her sister had cut off her beautiful long hair to a bob for this important visit. It pained Lata to see her thin shoulders hunched up in diffidence, her body held in a constant apologetic tension all the while she was there. She spoke freely only at night, whispering to Lata when they were alone. Savitri was gracious in receiving her father's gifts, fruit from their trees, plums, wild apples and walnuts, but beyond the initial pleasantries, she did not engage with them. Lata found little time alone with her father. He stayed close to Hukum, attentive, eager, constantly smiling. Lata felt embarrassed to see him reduced to this pitiable sight. Hukum did not ask for deference, but he received it easily, as though it was his due. Lata wished that her father could believe that his own kindness and gentleness gave him a worth and a place in this world. Lata could never make them feel comfortable in this house where she herself never felt she belonged. The visit wore her down. Her sister watched her like a hawk to report to her mother Lata's standing in this household. When they finally left, she felt both relieved and bereft. She knew that they would never truly be part of her world. Their departure marked an ending she had not felt even at the time of her marriage, as though a phase of her life was over.

Alone again at night, she lay awake and thought of Chandan for the first time in months. Even though he seemed insignificant now, she recalled his passionate kisses, the memory stirring her quietly as she pleasured herself. Despite the heat, she no longer opened the window at night.

The monsoon arrived, heavy and relentless, bringing much-needed relief from the summer's blaze. Rivers swelled and flooded in parts of the hills, and Lata worried for her parents' village, which experienced heavy landslides every year. Here, the rains painted a coat of green on the gentle slopes and threw a splash of blackish brown into the river. Every morning a spray of white mist hung over the valley, dissolving only when there was a heavy downpour. Lata enjoyed the change of scenery for a few days—wild monsoon blooms, droplets clinging to blades of grass, the damp, cool breeze. But soon the grey cloudy days began to weigh on her spirits. The women no longer went into the forest, and she had no one to speak to. She felt relieved when autumn came and the sun returned with a reduced intensity.

Hukum and Savitri were to go to Delhi to see their new-born grandson. There was a brief discussion about Lata accompanying them, but Savitri decided against it—hired help never looked after the cows properly. For the first time, Lata rose in anger, stormed to her room, and refused to hide her frustration. Savitri appeared not to notice, but the next morning, Lata found a new sari laid out on her bed—a quiet appeasement from Hukum. He also ensured the house was stocked with her favourite sweetmeats before they left.

It was calming to have the house to herself. The hired help, Basant, a poor relative of the family, was to come at night and assist during the day if needed. With the village women resuming their trips to the forest for fodder and firewood, Lata invited them over and served tea in the courtyard. They told Lata about the upcoming annual mela in the neighbouring village and it was decided that all of them would attend it together.

Basant came in early to take care of the house for the day, giving Lata time to get dressed at leisure. She took care to look her best, and rightly so, as all the women would be dressed in their brightest clothes. She wore the sari and jewellery Hukum had given her, and for that day she felt like a '*bade ghar ki bahu*', even though a nagging sense of guilt lingered, as if she knew that Hukum and Savitri would disapprove of her plans.

After a long walk to the bus stop and a considerable wait, the women got into an overcrowded bus, chattering excitedly as it rumbled toward the fairground.

Thousands of villagers had thronged the ground nestled in a cup of hills. Lata moved among them like a child, trying out every accessory, tasting treats from every food stall, and climbing on every ride.

Then there he was, leaning against a stall, looking at her with hurt eyes as if he had been waiting for her a long time. Lata broke away from the other women and rushed towards Chandan. And like an old song he brought back, in an instant, the remembrance of home. She stopped short of hugging him, taking his hand instead, struggling to contain the rush of affection mingled with guilt. He feigned surprise and indifference. He told her that he had left his studies and taken up a clerical job in Nainital Bank. She noted his sober clothes and the moustache that he wore uneasily on his soft face, as if it was his quiet declaration of the shift in his world after her marriage.

She suggested a ride on the Ferris wheel. He gallantly bought the tickets and candyfloss on a stick for the ride. Her heart skipped a beat as the wheel swung into motion, as if some possibilities had opened up in that moment. As they climbed up, he squeezed her hand tight and all the misery of the last few months streamed down his face and dripped in warm drops onto the back of her hand. She felt immobilised with the compassion that welled up in her heart. She looked at his bowed head and tears slipped unbidden down her own face. Up and down, the ferris wheel carried them, hands clasped, in a shared silence.

On the bus ride back, Lata sat away from the other women, wanting to be lost in her thoughts. She rested her head against the window letting the cool evening air sting her flushed cheeks. The setting sun had a bolder hue that day and the darkening hillsides seemed to fold around her in a softer embrace.

It was quite late when she got back, and a worried Basant was pacing around in the courtyard. She left him to lock up the house and went straight into her room. Lying on her bed, she gazed at the clear autumn night sky, listening to music, humming softly, lulled into a long-forgotten sense of freedom. Later she undressed before the rosewood cabinet mirror, pausing to look at herself, her long beautiful hair and her translucent skin. *She must see him again*, she thought, smiling to herself. He had told her that he had come all the way to the mela hoping to catch a glimpse of her and that he was staying with an acquaintance in a nearby village. She messaged him, asking him to meet her in the forest near her house. In his display picture he had his arm around a joker with a white face and a large red nose, both seated on a bench, the joker dressed in yellow overalls. She had been impressed when he had informed her that it was a photo outside an American restaurant during a visit to New Delhi.

She waited for him at the edge of the forest. When he was in sight, she began to move ahead, and he followed at a distance. No one from the village ventured into this part which adjoined Hukum Singh's property. Yet a pine forest with its tall bare trunks, sparse foliage and a complete absence of undergrowth, made her feel exposed. Every step, as she led him deep into the forest, was laden with anxiety. She found a bend near a stream and, seeing that it was well concealed by large rocks, allowed herself to relax into its secrecy.

The kisses were sweeter than she remembered. Revelling in his adoring gaze, she lay back on the rocks and looked up at the sky. The straight bare trunks of the pine trees seemed to converge above her, and through the neat clumps of foliage that capped them, sunlight filtered onto Lata's blissful face. *Isn't this all that she wanted?* she thought. To have the complete adoration of a man.

The next day she sent off Basant to the fair, pressing a generous tip into his hand and urging him to enjoy himself. Chandan had been hesitant about coming to the house but agreed when she assured him that her in-laws would be away for at least a couple of weeks. She was nervous too, yet intoxicated with a heady rush of passion.

She rose very early and finished all the housework. For the first time she felt as though the house truly belonged to her. Chandan arrived not through the main village but by the forest path, entering through the backyard. He immediately took a tour of the house and was quite surprised by the absence of modern comforts. He seemed more confident of himself that day. She stood behind him as he examined the photographs on the wall of her in-laws and of herself and Aalam on their wedding day.

She drew him into her room, where they made love through the day. They ate on her bed, and later she served him tea in the finest tea set taken out of the large wooden box in the kitchen. They spoke of the old days, which were more distant in her memory than they were in time. He gave her all the news of their friends in the village.

Sometime late in the afternoon, she heard a faint sound. She panicked and peered out of the window, calling out to Basant. But there was no response. She dressed quickly, glanced through the house, and finally convinced herself it was only a gust of wind. She returned to her room, not bothering even to shut the door.

Chandan lay on the bed, head propped on one elbow, looking increasingly withdrawn as the day wore on. She began to sing the Lata Mangeshkar songs he had once loved to hear her sing, hoping to elicit the old intensity of adoration, but she could sense him slipping away.

When he finally gathered himself to leave that evening, she clung to his neck, trying to draw some promise from him. He broke her grip with a strong shake of his head and stepped away. Lata's spirits began to sink.

As he dressed, he spoke of his girlfriend who was also his colleague. They planned to marry soon, he said. She was a graduate, had cleared a bank exam, and therefore held a position senior to his own. Lata was stung with this sudden revelation. She asked him if he would ever speak of what had passed between them. This did not count as betrayal, he replied and turned away.

She followed him into the courtyard. Bitter disappointment had dulled her senses, and she failed to register the sound coming from the kitchen. Her body trembled with humiliation as Chandan sauntered down the slope, never once stopping to look back. As she turned to go into the house, she noticed a thin wisp of smoke rising through the cracks between the ceiling stones.

The bolt of shock struck like a punch in her stomach. Had Basant returned early? Had he seen anything? Her mind was racing. She would tell him it was her cousin who had dropped by, that she was showing him photographs in her room. She climbed the stairs, nerves jangling, and slipped into her room. With shaking hands, she pulled out photo albums from her cupboard and scattered them across the bed. Then, gathering the cups and plates, she put on a nonchalant air and moved towards the kitchen, humming softly and calling out casually to Basant.

The long kitchen lay almost entirely in darkness. The shaft of light that entered through the open window turned into a smoky column because of the fire burning at the choolah. She peered into the darkness, calling out to Basant once more.

All she saw was the brief glint of a metal ladle as it caught the light. All she heard was the steady sound of it stirring and the pounding of her own heart. She called out again, this time in a frightened whisper and moved hesitantly towards the hearth.

By then her eyes had adjusted to the darkness. She discerned a tall figure crouched over the fire, stirring a pot of rice. Her heart lurched violently before turning to ice. A tongue of fire leapt up and lit Hukum's face. The tray slipped from her hands and clattered to the floor.

Hukum did not look up. He blew into the fire, sending embers and ash swirling in the air. She stood frozen for what felt like an interminable stretch of time, scarcely breathing. Only then did she understand that the faint sound she had heard earlier was him entering the house in his characteristic stealthy manner.

Hukum rose slowly to his full length and stepped into the smoky shaft of light. He struck a match and lit a bidi, blowing more smoke out through the window. And then he turned his grey-brown eyes to look at her.

She backed out of the kitchen and stumbled into her room. When the ringing in her ears subsided, all she could hear was her own breathing, loud and disembodied, as if it were outside her. Time slowed to a painful, agonising crawl. She heard every shuffle, every creak, every footstep. The house that had so briefly felt like her own had turned into a frightening trap.

When Basant returned that night, she crept to the door and strained to catch their voices. From their conversation she gathered that Hukum had been called back early by the forest department to hunt a man-eating leopard in the vicinity.

Lata lay awake for hours before sleep finally overtook her. She shivered through the night, not bothering to pull a covering over herself. The sound of the cows being brought in woke her up at dawn. She realised she had left them out all night. Unsure of how to begin the day, she turned the matter over in her mind again and again, eventually deciding to step out bravely into the courtyard.

Hukum was cleaning the cowshed. She could feel his eyes on her, but he said nothing. She went about her usual routine cautiously, all the while watching him with tense anticipation, like a wounded animal waiting for the hunter to strike. She wondered when he would go for the leopard hunt, but by evening she knew that he had already found his prey at home.

That night, as she lay on her bed, she heard him enter the room. She did not turn when he lay down behind her. Her body went cold and immobile. He pulled down her salwar and pushed into her with a dry, hard thrust as his rough hands slid up to her breasts. His stubble scraped her soft nape, and his grunts numbed her senses. When he was done and left, she remained where she was, staring into the darkness, unable to gather herself to get up and take a wash. His strong tobacco breath lingered on in the room long after dawn.

Autumn slipped into an early winter without warning. Hurried preparations had to be made before frost could dampen and spoil what was needed for the months ahead. Fire logs were stacked; cow fodder was gathered. Hired labour stocked the storeroom and cowshed with wood and raised lutas, tall mounds of hay built around a single pole, standing stiffly against the cold.

Lata threw herself into the work with a blind, punishing fervour, driving her body to extreme exhaustion. It ensured that after enduring Hukum, who came into her room every other night, she fell into a thick and dreamless sleep. She refused to dwell on how her body had begun to betray her on those cold winter nights, responding despite her will. Nor would she allow herself to think about the other silence that had crept in, the months slipping by without blood.

Savitri made no comment on the prized tea set's missing pieces when she returned from Delhi. It was impossible for Lata to tell how much she knew, for she herself had stopped meeting anyone's eyes. She did not even look at her own reflection in the mirror. She avoided sitting down to meals with them, eating instead alone in her room or out in the courtyard. She kept away from the village women altogether and spoke very little even to her parents and sisters. She knew they were worried, but she could not bring herself to reassure them. Her father had called Hukum once, who told them that everything was all right.

Lata had hoped that her extreme exertions would bring on a miscarriage, but when winter gave into summer, she could not ignore the tight bulge of her tummy.

When Aalam called to inform them that he would soon be home on his annual leave, she decided to draw Savitri into the situation. When Hukum was away, Lata went into the kitchen and called out to her mother-in-law in a rough, rude voice. She stood in the doorway showing her bulging profile. Savitri's eyes went first to her stomach and then, lifted to Lata's face, looking at her directly for the first time. A cold fear passed between them. But Savitri said nothing and turned her back on Lata.

The following day Lata cornered Hukum in the cowshed and forced him to look at her growing stomach. When he didn't respond at once, she shoved his shoulder with impatience and urgency. He turned his steely eyes on her and told her to take care of it before Aalam arrived. Without another word he strode out of the cowshed and into the fields.

She stood where he had left her, her feet rooted to the ground. *Take care of it.* She had already tried drinking ajwain water and had shaken and punched her belly with her hands, but nothing had worked. She spun into action and walked with purpose towards the work shed to prepare for the operation, arranging a bed of hay for herself and bringing in a *saria*, a long metal rod with a pointed tip, which she stood against the wall. She hardly cared how dangerous her plan was considering how far gone she was into her pregnancy.

When she went again into the shed that night, the cows mooed in protest. Not bothering to be silent, she lay down on the bed of hay, feeling nothing, intent only on getting the job done. She picked up the saria and inserted it into her vagina. She repeatedly pushed it in with as much force as she had the courage to muster.

She lay for hours in the cowshed, groaning in pain, the night passing slowly around her. She could hear them shuffling in the room above. At dawn Savitri came down with tea and water, paused at the threshold, then turned away without a word, not wanting to participate any more in Lata's shame. Hukum had left already for work. It was only by afternoon that it was over.

Lata gathered everything into an old blanket. She thought that the bloody foetus had moved with life for a few seconds before going still. She left the bundle in the cowshed and went into the bathroom to clean herself, scrubbing each part of her body meticulously. Disregarding the rule that she was 'untouchable' for a few days and could not go into the kitchen, she stormed in and sat right next to the choolah. Her hair hung loose and her eyes had a wild look. She served herself a hearty meal and ate while watching the wood collapse into glowing cinders, the sharp crackle ringing through the disquiet around her.

Savitri peered in and caught sight of her. She stood in the doorway, staring in disbelief, but when Lata turned her hollow eyes on her she recoiled and fled, as if she had seen a demon.

When dusk fell, and after she heard the women returning from the forest, Lata picked up the dripping bundle and walked down to the jacaranda tree, once again heavy with bloom. The saria was now used to dig a deep hollow into the mauve carpet of fallen flowers. She began to unwrap the bundle, ready to empty out the contents into the earth, when all at once something long dormant stirred in her heart, and she stopped.

Though it was summer, the night air was chilly. She swaddled the dead foetus carefully again, tucking the blanket around it before lowering it into the soil. She looked up at the canopy of the tree against the inky sky, searching for that twisted branch that had taken life from Malti Amma's baby all those years ago. Everything seemed alive for a moment. She sat in the still summer night for a long time thinking of absolutely nothing. At last she covered the grave with soft dark earth and light mauve flowers.

She locked the door and windows of her room and slept almost continuously for the next two days. Savitri knocked on her door a few times but she did not respond. She remembered that Aalam was due to arrive the following day. What were they going to do with her then? What lies would they tell Aalam about her? She could hear them conspiring in hushed tones outside her room.

When the house fell silent, she opened her window and looked out into the moonless night. The soft drone of the crickets, the stillness of the dark shadows and the flat black outlines of the mountains against the sky began to close in on her. She breathed rhythmically.

Her eyes were drawn to the jacaranda tree, its pale blooms faintly luminous in the dark. Except they were not flowers; they were eyes, lifted towards her. Many eyes. Alive. The darkness surged forward to envelop her in its embrace. Sinking into its warmth, her gaze drifted to the path, faintly discernible, her escape from this life. Her eyes then travelled up to the heavy wooden beams holding up the ceiling and to the heavy wood furniture around her.

She bent down and picked up a jerrycan from beneath her bed. Unscrewing the cap, she tipped it and watched the kerosene wander along the wooden ramparts of the room, a dark sheen drinking into grain and crack. She paused, listening to the house holding its breath, to the soft, distant snores of lives sealed away elsewhere. The thick silence settled again. She struck a match.

Outside, she drew the heavy door shut, bolted it from the night-facing side, and stepped away as the flames flared up.

Gangrene

It started as a tiny wound. He rolled the small round stone between his fingers after pinching it out from under the skin on the side of his big toenail. It had probably lodged itself during the blasting in the quarry. He had gone around the corner for a piss and was caught unawares by a deafening explosion. He had clamped his hands to his ears as a sharp ringing pierced through his head. When it subsided, he found that a fine sheath of dust had covered him completely, but he had not felt this grain of rock going into his skin. Flicking it away, he continued to wash the dirt off himself thoroughly. A sluggish river of mud slithered down the drain that cut across the light grey stone courtyard.

The summer months still afforded some light when he got back home before the valley plunged into darkness. Umed Singh slurped at the sugary tea, his tall, lean form squatting on the parapet of the courtyard, weighed down by the fifty-six years on him. With his free hand, he brushed off the limestone dust from his short-cropped wavy hair, which was still surprisingly jet black. The increasing gauntness of his face made his chiselled features and aquiline nose more prominent. His forehead was deeply furrowed by hours of labour in the sharp sun adding, along with the slight downward slant of his deep-set eyes, a tragic note to his countenance. Finishing his tea, he continued to stare ahead blankly at the dry yellow-green valley that sloped down gently to a river. Ija, his mother, moved around silently behind him in the low double-storied stone house with a roof of slate tiles. It was the only occupied house in this valley and was surrounded by terraced fields and immense silence.

A burst of distant laughter made Umed shift his gaze to the row of houses above on the far-left side of the mountain. He could see small silhouettes of children playing against the sky. But the mirth died down quickly, swallowed by the long layers of fields between them.

Lyat Singh sat on a foldable nylon armchair in his courtyard, his crossed legs giving him an air of authority. He looked at the unchanging desolate valley ahead of him, the emptiness broken only by the small yellowish section of the limestone quarry that was visible on this side of the mountain. Deep stirrings of dissatisfaction aggravated his temper, and he snapped at his grandchildren who were squealing with glee while rolling in the dirt. Even if it meant giving up his principalship of the Government Intercollege, he thought, he had to move out in the coming year. No one worth anything was left in the village. If only Umed Singh would agree to leasing his land to the quarry contractor, he would be able to do so too. It would mean a decent income from the land that they were not cultivating anymore. Looking scornfully at his wife who, her sari hitched up to her knees, insisted on cultivating a small patch of land for vegetables, he called out, 'How many diamonds have you dug out already?'

As night rapidly descended, he got up to go in, glancing below at the ghostly rows of deserted houses. His gaze shifted down further to Umed's hazy figure disappearing into the darkness of his lone house as his mother hovered in the courtyard calling in the cows.

The exaggerated shadows thrown by the blazing kitchen fire on the mud walls were deceptively animated before they died down suddenly. The logs hissed as water quenched the fire and smoke enveloped the kitchen. The blurred dark forms of Umed and Ija as they squatted on the kitchen floor seemed almost still. Ija's soft grunt, as she dropped an extra lump of ghee on a thick roti in Umed's plate, evoked no response from him.

He flexed his feet, stretched his neck over the edge of the narrow hard bed, and was soon lulled into sleep to the low sound of the television. Beyond his cell-like room Ija crouched on the mud floor in the kitchen extension, watching a small television screen. It was a reminder of her daughter who had bought it for her on her last visit two years ago. She died of jaundice a few months later. They had called Ija to take care of her, but she did not go. She didn't go for the funeral either, nor did Umed. Her family had not spoken to them since. Ija was losing her hearing, and her eyesight was almost killed by those dark blobs that had appeared in her eyes and were slowly but surely spreading their tentacles. She watched the coloured shadows more as atonement for her daughter's death than for any fascination with them.

Outside in the dark fields the chirping of crickets ebbed and flowed in the thick warm silence.

Umed was peering into a small cracked mirror as he shaved when he became aware of a mild throbbing pain in his right toe. He washed it with water, and that was that. He ate his morning meal in the courtyard while Ija went about her chores. No words were exchanged except for her telling him to buy sugar on his way back from work. Slipping his feet into mud-encrusted rubber slippers, Umed set off on the long walk to the quarry, which was on the other side of the mountain to his right. He wore a loose pale blue kurta-pyjama and, even though it was hot, a ragged sleeveless sweater, keeping in mind the capricious weather in the mid-Himalayan ranges. The walk would have taken him twenty minutes when he was younger and was accustomed to loping up and down these slopes, but now it took quite a bit longer. Ija was never comfortable with him working in the quarry—in fact, she had been one of the few to oppose the quarry coming up near their village and had resisted leasing out her fields for mining. The villagers were surprised when Umed had started working there, but he himself thought little of it. Even though the quarry contractors offered less than the stipulated daily wage, it was steady work for six to seven months; certainly more comfortable than going up to the market and looking for odd jobs.

His tall body, stooped in submission, cut across and up the narrow dirt path with a long regular gait through dark green clumps of trees and overgrown terraced fields. As he neared the top of the hill, he paused just a moment under the shade of an oak tree to catch a whiff of a cool breeze blowing uphill, then quickening his pace he crossed over to the other side.

Hot dry air hit him as he began descending into a dramatically different vista. The limestone quarry was like an open festering wound, extending right down the steep mountain face, eating into the landscape as far as the eye could see. Scattered unevenly on its pale yellow earth were dark red pits of magnesite deposits. On its top edges stood a thick line of trees, shocking in their greenness, like a scab on the wound.

The grating noise of loading trucks and heavy drills echoed in the hollow of the quarry. As Umed headed towards the flat clearing where the labourers had gathered, a sudden gust of wind whipped up a cloud of dust that swallowed him in a white shroud.

The sun dragged itself overhead as the men laboured in the heat and dust. A loud siren echoed off the bare walls, bringing work to a halt. While the others sought out the scanty pockets of shade the quarry offered, Umed crossed over back to the other side of the mountain and headed down the gentle yellow-green slope towards a small stone temple. Even though it was a considerable walk, he liked to come away every afternoon during the break. He sat down against the outer stone wall of the temple under the shade of a horse chestnut tree.

Lighting a bidi, he inspected his right toe. The wound had begun to fester, and the toe had swelled up. He pressed it against the ground, feeling a small sharp pain, which was followed by a sweet throbbing. He continued to put pressure on it as he rested in the deep silence of the warm afternoon, watching a thin thread of smoke rising from the gaps in the stone roof of his house. Ija was cooking the evening meal. He heard a soft breeze sighing up from the river far below and setting the dry grass into a faint rustle. Then it moved past him into the patch of forest above, and Umed waited to hear the hard oak leaves flutter into a metallic cadence. This unchanging rhythm of the breeze gave him a deep sense of calm, as if everything were in its place. But he was not consciously aware of this feeling himself and, if compelled to articulate it, would have said that it was a day like so many countless days in his life. He pressed his toe again, and a bud of clear discharge popped up, followed by a palpable throbbing. He spotted a train of ants carrying a dead grasshopper towards the root of the chestnut tree. In the bright light, it seemed as if the grasshopper was floating through the air. Once the cuckoos started, they went on for a long time, and the summer air became dense with their urgent yet monotonous mating calls. This always had a soporific effect on Umed, but he shook off the feeling and headed back to the quarry.

Sundar twisted the plastic bag containing sugar and tied the top into a knot. Umed had seen Lyat Singh sitting on a wooden bench outside the ration-cum-teashop with two village elders. When he called out and offered him a cup of tea, Umed knew what it was about. While he wanted to avoid the usual course of these conversations, it was not in his nature to confront or offend. He accepted the tea reluctantly and sat down on his haunches against a stone pillar.

Lyat's tone was condescending. 'You must have given the matter a thought by now and discussed it with your Ija?'

Umed gave him a noncommittal nod, let out a soft grunt and then looked fixedly at the ground as he sipped his tea.

'Only if you agree will I be able to lease out my land for quarrying. Don't you see your house is right in the middle, there is no way around that,' Lyat said with rising impatience.

Khim Singh, a mild-mannered old man, was sitting on a bench, hunched up over his thigh. Taking a long drag from his bidi, he spoke in the deep, heavy voice of a lifelong smoker, 'His Ija does not want to see all the fields destroyed. It's all she's ever known in her life.'

'Well, he is working with the quarry anyway, digging other people's land, so what is the big deal? It is going to happen sooner or later; the contractors will use every trick to get all of us out.'

Lyat got up and started pacing about. Umed gave him a quick look, finished his tea in a single gulp and, without making eye contact with anyone, started to move away. Lyat went after him and shoved his shoulder in a hostile manner. He was shouting now.

'Look at me! I am the principal of an intercollege and yet I want to move out, leave my government job if necessary. What are you doing? Labour-giri! Has there been any change in your life in the last fifty years? The world has moved ahead, brother. You can have a better life in the plains ... you could go and stay with your daughter ... her husband has a decent government job. There is nothing left here. Your land does not even produce enough to feed you. Limestone is the only wealth this land has—take it!'

Umed continued to move down the slope.

Lyat called out desperately, 'The lease is only for five years. You can take it back then if you like.'

Khim let out a sigh, 'What will be left of that land after five years?'

He looked at Sundar, who was leaning on the shop counter, and let out an uneasy laugh. No one felt comfortable opposing Lyat directly—he carried the authority that every schoolmaster has in these parts.

Lyat gave Khim a sharp look. 'In time everything will grow back.'

'It cannot on its own, it will need healing,' Khim said, looking at the sky now with feigned concentration.

Irritated, Lyat snapped at Sundar, 'I would advise you to move as well. What are you doing selling biscuits and tea here? You can have a larger shop in the plains. We paharis have no ambition, that is why we get left behind.'

Khim got up at this point and moved into the shop. 'Sundar is minting money. The quarry labour is giving him rent and eating his food. Times are good for him.'

Lyat snatched his bag from the bench and headed off, muttering to himself angrily.

A few days later, the wound had become harder to ignore. It was full of pus, and the throbbing had become a sharp pain. Umed pressed the tender and swollen toe, clamping his thumb down on the wound and clenching his teeth against the excruciating pain, letting go only when there was no more white discharge. He doubled up in agony as the unbearable pain in his toe and the stab that rang between his ears took a while to subside. After washing the foot with cold water and cleaning it with a rag, he set off for work. He was a little breathless as he laboured up the hillside. The wound was making him hobble a little, but he soon got used to the rhythm of putting less weight on his right foot.

As days passed, he began to feel tired in the first half of the day and started giving up the extra walk for his afternoon siesta. The toe was turning purple, and Umed often found himself gently pressing down on it to feel the sharp pain go up his leg, waiting for the palpable pleasure when it faded. A fellow worker suggested that he cover up the wound—all the dust going into it couldn't be good. Umed looked around and spotted the remnants of an old white plastic sack lying near him and tore a strip with his teeth. After dusting it with his hand, in a half-hearted attempt to clean it, he wrapped it around the wound in a tight knot. It gave him some relief, and he carried on with the day's work.

The night was warm and stifling. Rolling around restlessly, Umed threw away the cover and tried to ward away various thoughts that had begun to creep back into his head. The toe did not hurt anymore, but the pain had moved up to his ankle, a constant throbbing pain that was no longer pleasurable. There was a faint smell of rotting flesh that trailed him, and he stooped down to sniff his toe to confirm the source. He hobbled to the kitchen and poured himself cool water from the clay pot. The foot made him clumsy, and the steel glass fell from his hand and thudded on the mud floor. Umed saw that Ija, who was lying on the floor like a heap of clothes, did not stir. He was grateful that she could barely hear anymore.

He lay down again and turned his head towards the window to look out at the dark, inky sky, littered with a multitude of stars. It struck him that he was looking at it after a long time, perhaps after decades. If he looked long enough, the stars seemed to be embedded in the blackness, and then as he continued to stare unblinkingly, they would pop out of it. Finally, he fell into a well of uneasy rest.

As the sky opened its eye, Umed emerged from a deafening dreamscape to the silence of the morning around him. Earlier, it would have been a relief to wake up. Earlier he would have worried about what the visions might portend. But in the past few years he had begun to savour the adventure and excitement his nightmares offered as the unchanging nature of his life had lulled his anxieties. He knew the details would slip away soon, so he closed his eyes again to recollect them.

He was looking down at terraced fields of jet-black crop that swayed ever so slightly. A white gleaming path wound around the fields, forming a sort of maze—his dreams were usually in black and white. Ija was in the fields trying to ask him something, but all he could hear was the faint whisperings of the crop. His sister was calling out to Ija from the other end of the fields. He looked up to see a thick sheet of water rolling down towards them from the top of a mountain, making a loud grating sound ... or was that from another dream ... he was not sure. They needed to run, or they would drown in the river that was filling the valley. But he could not move. Someone was pulling him into the house which was like a cavern. He turned to see that it was his beautiful daughter who had clasped his hand. Next to her stood her toad-like husband. Even in his dream he had thought ruefully that she deserved better, and a deep sense of regret continued to linger when he woke up.

The end of the dream was a jumbled-up profusion of images and emotions, and with a sigh he let it fade away. Even though the settings of his dreams were usually around his house, the details of the landscape and, more importantly the light, was dramatically different from one dream to the next. He pondered over this unresolvable mystery as he looked out of his window at the familiar fields, at the unchanged panorama on this side of the mountain.

As he hobbled down to the courtyard, the pain in his leg returned immediately. He opened the bandage and saw that his big toe had turned black. He tried to move it, but it was numb. He pulled at it, and it came right off in his grasp, black and rotting.

For a long moment, he simply stared at that piece of himself unbelievingly, his breath trapped in his throat, and then with a gasp he jerked it away. The toe landed under an orange tree. There was a putrid smell in the air. *I must go to the hospital in the next town immediately*, he told himself, as his breath rasped through flamed nostrils. *But the hospitals have long queues, and it will take me at least four days to get back. How can I leave Ija by herself and ... what if the doctor decides to cut off the leg?* Umed took a deep breath and calmed himself. *It's just a toe*, he reasoned, *I can do without it. I'll put a bandage of turmeric on it tonight and now that the rotten bit has fallen off, it will heal.* He said nothing to Ija and headed out for work at his usual time.

The hot sun made Umed dizzy, and he had to step out of the human chain hauling sacks of limestone into a truck. He began to stagger up and out of the pit using a shortcut, but the loose earth made him slip down back into the hollow. He used the path that led out of the pit and, half-crawling, half-walking, managed to reach a stony unshaded rockface and collapsed onto it. Sick to his gut, he tried to catch his breath and get a hold on himself, using his hands to shield his head from the cruel sun. The pain ate into his leg, right up to the hip. He pulled up the pyjama leg to see that the skin was bubbling, fermenting and the rot was seeping up. He gulped down hot air through his gaping mouth, squinting at the workers milling far below him in the wide festering pit. Like a squad of trained ants carrying the flesh of the earth. The overseer, wearing a helmet, was talking to one of the labourers and pointing at him. He could feel the accusatory look from afar, and Umed knew that his wages would be docked if he didn't get back to work immediately.

But as soon as he gathered himself, he found himself rolling down the slippery limestone slope, coming to a stop only when the workers ran towards him and held him. He had a fever and was asked to leave. He had no memory of how he got home, only of the sympathetic voice of a fellow labourer assuring him that some rest would cure him.

Umed lay down on the cool courtyard stones and fell into a tired slumber. He woke up to the sound of a blast in the quarry. He raised himself on his elbows to look at the limestone dust in the sky and the pain shot up his leg, a thick hot rod grinding into his knee and then dulling into an ache as it moved up. His breath was burning and he was unable to pick himself off the floor immediately. He dragged himself to the ledge and propped himself against it. He looked for his toe under the orange tree. He did not spot it immediately but then there it was, standing up against the dark trunk, alive with ants crawling all over it. He managed to stumble up to his room and lay down on his bed.

Ija hadn't realised he was home until late in the evening. She put a cold compress on his feverish forehead and tried to fuss over him as best as she could. She wondered about the putrid smell. He said nothing to her, but she investigated and discovered the missing toe. He appeased her, saying he would go to the hospital as soon as he was better. She brought out the rum and they both took a shot of it. It made him feel better, and he splashed some of it on the wound too. Later, Ija covered the wound with turmeric paste. He urged her to watch some television and go to sleep. He slept better that night, the smell did not bother him anymore; he had grown used to it. But the next morning the fever was back. He convinced Ija to go to the fields and work, and that he would be fine.

He came out into the courtyard in the hot afternoon, shivering and feeling confused. He noticed that his toe had disappeared from under the orange tree. After he had soaked in some sun, his skin began to burn and the blasts in the quarry set off a severe headache. He dipped his head into a bucket of cold water. The hospital was fifty kilometres away, and it was a long walk to the roadhead where he would get a bus or a jeep. *Why did I stay back in this god-forsaken place? Someone had to be with Ija, didn't they?* He could still see her looking at him from the window as his father's dead body lay in the courtyard. It had been a relief for Umed, that death. His father had a frightening temper and was urging Umed to join the army like him. But Umed never wanted to leave Ija, never wanted to leave the village. His thoughts wandered as he continued to sweat onto the courtyard stones.

It seemed like someone else's life that he remembered—another person in another time. The place was unchanged but time had moved through it. His wife lay in the same courtyard, her face beautiful even in death, his young daughter clinging to her mother's lifeless form. She looked like him, the daughter, sharp and tall. No, he had no vanity for himself but often regretted giving his beautiful daughter to that ape of a man just because he had a government job. And that ape was ashamed of them, never visited them anymore, and told everyone that his father-in-law was the quarry contractor. At least the grandchildren had his daughter's looks, all except the youngest.

He turned his head towards the hot fields, hoping to catch a whiff of breeze to ease the suffocation he felt. But the only movement in that stillness was his own burning breath. He felt a knot in his stomach as he spotted a python wrapped on a birch tree about fifteen metres away from him, its pale body well camouflaged on the white bark. Unblinking marble eyes watched Umed, its scales heaving almost imperceptibly as it strengthened its hold on the tree. Then it went as still as death and waited patiently.

Umed let the cuckoo calls put him to sleep that day. When he woke up, he was in extreme pain. He peeled back his pyjama leg. Bits of skin were stuck to the cloth. He ripped his shirt off, tore away a sleeve and tied it tightly just above his knee. As the pain subsided, so did the ringing in his head, and the racket of the crickets took over as evening fell. The snake was gone. *Had it crept into the house?* Umed looked fearfully at the long columns of darkness that the doors opened into. He dragged himself to his room, pulling his numb leg behind him.

He heard Ija's soothing voice and opened his eyes. The pitch-black night outside startled him. He panicked and told her to shut all the doors and windows. But she was far away; only her hand at the end of a long arm was caressing his forehead. Her distant voice whispered endearments into his ear... her handsome unfortunate son ... he must not work in the quarry anymore ... if it was winter it would have been alright, the wound would have healed. Umed refused to eat, and finally Ija left the room, not able to tolerate the stench.

The calm morning had a feeling of finality. It felt like the day his daughter got married ... like the day he himself got married ... like the morning after his father died. As he got off the bed, his right leg just sank into the ground, completely numb. He dragged it down the narrow wooden staircase and into the courtyard. He laid it in front of him. It had turned a deep blue up to his knee. After a moment's hesitation, he pulled at it—and with a squishy sound, it came off in his grasp, right off from his knee. He looked at that rotten piece of limb he was holding. He was seized with real panic for the first time—*perhaps it had gone too far.* Then came a feeling of defiance, and he cried out aloud, 'Let it go; I can function with one leg.' Almost choking from the stench, he flung it as far as he could with all the might left in his body. He inspected the wound left behind, a yellow, festering wound with raw pits of blood. A vulture began to hover above the field where his leg lay, gliding smoothly in wide circles. Umed's eyes followed it.

He crawled into the cowshed so Ija wouldn't see him and get terrified. He lay in the dry hay with nothing to mark the time except the coming and going of a fever. *It will all be okay, we have Ija's pension to fall back on,* he thought over and over again. His head sank into the haystack. A loud blast went off in the quarry. He lay there all day and night. He had a flash of himself going over the hill to collect firewood with his little sister. They went deep into the thick forest where the quarry now was. They caught ladybirds and put them into a steel tumbler stuffed with nettles. His sister collected juicy hishalus, yellow berries from laden bushes, and they ate them sitting next to the stream, the stream that had disappeared, the forest that was erased. Before going home, they released the ladybirds, but most of them had to be coaxed to fly away.

The next morning Ija found him dead. She walked all the way to the market to call the villagers. They looked hard for the missing leg but could not find it. Many suggested that the soul would not find peace if the leg was not burnt along with the body. Lyat tried to talk to Ija about leasing out her land to the quarry contractors, but she simply responded by repeating over and over again that if it had been winter, the wound would have healed.

In the months that followed the blasts from the quarry continued to ring in the valley through the day. At night Ija started keeping the volume of the television very low so that she could hear the sound of the foot that paced in the courtyard.

The Man Who Refused to Die

In the vast expanse of the dry river bed, the dark figures of the mourners were scattered amidst big white boulders. Shanti, looking down at them from the village above, clutched her sleeping baby to her breast, comforted by his warm, soft breath on her neck, keenly feeling both the dread and relief one feels when a grave tragedy has befallen someone else. As a sudden gust of wind scraped the wheat ears in the fields, Shanti turned away to go inside her house. The baby had a mild cold which could worsen in this sudden turn of weather.

The young man's body lay on a sandy patch, right under the precipice he had fallen from. Blood had seeped into the white sand. Walking back home on a steep slope the night before, hopelessly drunk, he did not live to learn that danger could lurk even on a familiar path. His mother busied herself with covering each part of him with a dark blanket, diligently offering protection to the cold body, delaying the acceptance of the finality of his death.

Beyond, on the edge of the river bed, gigantic rusted metal pipes were strewn haphazardly. Foliage had crept around and between them, tempering their oddity in this remote valley, slowly erasing the evidence of the corruption that had fattened several pockets before the hydel project was abandoned altogether. Above the denuded hillside, which indicated the depth and fury of the river when it raged in the monsoons, thickly forested slopes rose darkly into the whiteness of snow-capped mountains and, that day, fittingly, a grey sky.

The mother finally let out a piercing howl which was swallowed by the icy wind that swept through the valley and carried away into the emptiness ahead of them created by the sudden fall in the river's path. She looked towards the sky and begged for her life to be taken instead of his. The other women began wailing too, beating their chests, grabbing at the dead boy's stiff limbs to express their sorrow. This was followed, inevitably, by muted conversation amongst the men about the fickleness of destiny, which snatched away some in their prime while continuing to spare the others.

Here their eyes turned to Kushal Baba, an ancient-looking ascetic, who sat under a gnarled tree at some distance from them, and watched the body with a fixed, impassive gaze, drawing deep puffs from his bidi. He was wrapped in a dark rough shawl under which orange robes hung loosely over his skeletal body. The smear of sandalwood paste was visible on his deeply furrowed brow, and his matted dreadlocks were bundled on the top of his head. Despite his advancing years, he never missed an occasion of mourning in the village. He was more than a hundred years old, it was believed. He smoked and drank with vigour, had no near and dear ones to miss him, and yet shuffled on from one year into another, mysteriously bouncing back after every ailment.

In her inconsolable anguish, feeling acutely the deep injustice of fate, the dead boy's mother watched him as he got up and began to move slowly up the hillside on his way back to the village, continuing to consume time on this earth while her son, barely in his twenties, lay stiff, bereft of a life that should rightfully have been his.

It happened whenever there was a death. Amidst talk of how each life was apportioned a certain number of breaths, seconds and even grains to eat, of the wisdom of not measuring the worth of a life by its longevity, between the debate of whether death reaffirms our faith in life or if it makes it meaningless, at some point all eyes would be on Kushal Baba. Nothing was said, but the unfair balance of the situation was felt, especially by the grieving family who had lost someone who was invariably younger than Kushal Baba. Some attributed his long life to his asceticism, but it was evident to everyone that apart from the orange robes, there was nothing spiritual about him. Unlike other people, Kushal Baba never offered any consolation to the bereaved family. In fact, there was never a flicker of emotion on his face.

It was sinister, his silence, thought Shanti as she soothed her sick baby, sitting out in her sunny courtyard. A couple of weeks had passed since the young boy's death, and the air of gloom in the village had begun to dispel somewhat. But Shanti herself was worried and restless. Her baby was sick. His fever had not broken for the last one week. She had tried all local remedies from herbal pastes and concoctions to jhad-phoonk. Nothing had worked. There were no medical facilities near the village where she could take her child.

Shanti's husband worked in the city, and the rest of the family had migrated to a small town nearby. She had to stay back in the village to look after the house and fields, much to her relief. But now she looked uneasily at the increasing bare patches on the snow-clad mountains and at the barren fields around her. There had been very little rainfall this year. Across the hill a motorable road ended in a landslide of rubble, like a yellow gash across the green hills. Governments had come and gone, making promises of progress and development, but all that remained was a sterile silence and the jaundiced look of desolation caused by increasing dust in the air. Below the village stood the facade of a hospital which was inaugurated with much fanfare almost a decade ago, but, again, the project was abandoned. Maybe it was time to hasten a move to the city for the sake of her baby, Shanti thought, instead of clinging on to memories of a softer existence that had been her childhood, spent in these parts when they were lush and green.

The sun was burning a hazy ring in the sky. Shanti turned to wipe the sweat trickling down her neck when she was startled by the sight of Kushal Baba standing outside the courtyard, watching her and the baby. He lived beyond her fields and often went by her house. But today the sight of his reed-like figure, the stillness with which he held his form, and the vacant gaze with which he seemed to be looking at her child set her heart racing. He stood a moment longer and then moved on with a slow and measured gait. Shanti continued to watch him. Like a bolt of lightning, a realisation struck her, leaving her body tingling and her stomach in a frightening churn.

Kushal Baba ate the lives of others! That is how he kept escaping the jaws of death! Shanti sat still, her heart thumping, her breath shallow, trying to think through the rationale of her epiphany. Only a few months ago he had been very ill. The villagers had started making arrangements for his funeral when he miraculously recovered, and a younger man in the village, in his fifties and with no known ailment, died all of a sudden. She began feverishly connecting all the recent and unexpected deaths in the village to Kushal Baba, more and more convinced of her own reasoning.

Suddenly feeling vulnerable out in the open, she picked up the baby and ran into the house. She put him down on the bed and frantically slammed all the doors and windows shut, hoping to shield the house from the negative energy that she believed lingered outside. The baby whimpered, hearing the loud bangs. She rushed to him and held him close. She was afraid that the long journey to the nearest hospital would be uncomfortable for him, but everyone had been advising her that she should not delay it as his condition was deteriorating and he had stopped feeding completely. But now she knew no matter what she did, the baby would not survive because Kushal Baba was drawing the life out of him.

As Shanti continued to crush the baby to her chest, Kushal Baba's evil gaze, the subtle shift of his eyes from her to her baby, ran like a loop in her head. She tried to remember when he had come to the village ... it was about ten or fifteen years ago. He was already very old, and the villagers had welcomed him warmly, believing that an ascetic residing in their village would mean that prosperity and abundance would follow. They had got together and communally built a small stone house for him. Even though he had enjoyed their generosity, were there not rumours about him being in cahoots with the wood mafia? And hadn't she heard stories of the village women complaining of being asked for unreasonable favours when they visited him? After he had entered the village, disharmony and disputes had erupted between families, and floods had regularly ravaged the valley. Shanti continued to make her case against him firmly. The villagers did not have it in them to drive him away, but she must do something before his hungry gaze consumed her precious child. Her child who had not even begun to walk. Her child who was born to her with so much difficulty after seven years of marriage.

It was getting dark outside. The sky rumbled loudly. Soon rain began pelting down on the slate tiles of the roof, making an unusual din. A large drop of water dripped onto the baby's forehead in a loud splat, reminding Shanti of the crack in the roof tile that she had meant to fix but hadn't been able to yet because of his ill health. She moved him to another part of the bed and placed a bucket under the leak.

In a fresh wave of sympathetic love, she kissed his face repeatedly, whispering urgently to him to stay alive for a few hours, that everything would be okay and that she had made up her mind to take care of the situation. Kushal Baba went to the fields very early every morning, even before the break of dawn, for his ablutions. He was not comfortable with the modern toilets that had recently been introduced to the village. That was her chance. Before he could eat up her baby, she would finish him off. She felt no fear, in fact she felt very calm once she knew how she would save her child.

The rain had abated. Shanti lay awake, patting the baby's back now and again to make sure he was still alive, and when he whimpered in affirmation, she would return to counting every drop of water that fell into the bucket, like the ticking of an uneven clock. She got out of bed well before the crack of dawn, kissed the baby's forehead and crept out into the cold and wet night. She climbed onto the roof from the elevated field adjoining it and positioned herself just above the path that went past her house, the path that Kushal Baba would take to the fields.

Clutching a sickle in her hand, she lay down flat on the ice-cold slate roof. Her body shivered violently as she struggled to keep herself as still and focused as possible. She would pounce on him as he passed by—neither too early nor too late. If she could jump on him without him seeing her, she would be able to pin him down and, while he was still in shock, slit his throat. She would drag his body to the fields and leave it for wild animals to take care of before the rest of the village was up. However, she was not too concerned about the consequences of getting discovered. All that mattered was that she save her little boy.

She did not have to wait too long before she saw a form, wrapped in a dark blanket, shuffling down the path and moving towards her house. She recognised Kushal Baba. The sight of him stoked the fear and hatred she felt so keenly, and she had to hold herself back from springing up too early. She measured her breaths, slowly drawing in the cold air to calm her racing heart. Just as he was under her, she rose to her full height, holding the sickle above her head.

Right at that moment Kushal Baba turned his head. He saw her dark form against the sky, ready for attack.

All Shanti saw in the darkness were the ghostly whites of Kushal Baba's eyes which had rolled upwards to look at her. There was a loud, sharp snap followed by an almost silent fall. The cracked stone tile on the roof caved in under Shanti, taking her down with the entire section of the roof which crashed with great force into the house below, onto the bed that the sick baby lay in.

At the funeral, people sighed and talked of how a fixed number of breaths were apportioned to every life and how no one could change that. Shanti sat on her haunches, her gaze pinned to the ground. In a dark corner, Kushal Baba stood staring at the dead child while the rest of the village mourned.

When it was over, the body was lifted and carried away. Someone swept the floor clean. Kushal Baba shuffled back to his house across the fields.

By evening, the villagers had returned to work.

A Long Way Home

Shekhar Pant hurriedly handed his I-card and road permit to the cop who was leaning in impatiently through the car window, his facemask hanging carelessly around his neck. He suspiciously observed Shekhar's delicate features, his fair skin that was somewhat puffy and sagging with ill health rather than age.

'The hills are yet free of the disease, and you want to carry it here?' he roared.

'My mother is critically ill … I have travelled all the way from Mumbai to see her.' Shekhar replied, feeling more fraudulent than necessary.

'But your permit is only till Kathgodam.' He thumped the car top and barked, 'Chalo, turn it around.'

As the car started, he climbed onto his scooter and, in a great rush to get somewhere, disappeared around the bend. Shekhar ordered the driver to continue, reminding him of the exorbitant amount he was charging for this journey, hoping there would be no more checks after that point.

As they left the foothills, the fairly broad road wrapped itself around the hills, gently working its way up. Shekhar looked at the pine forests with unfamiliar eyes. Large sections of hillsides had been ravaged by landslides, and the building of this tarred road had altered the perspective with which one viewed the valley. The bare pine trunks that scrolled by in an almost perfect rhythm lulled his anxiety, and he fell into a distracted slumber. His head slumped back over the seat top and bright sunlight through the rear window lit his face, so when the car swung around a sharp curve and woke him, his eyes still carried red, blurry remnants of sunlight.

The road had become narrower and steeper as they climbed higher. The cold crisp air revived his tired nerves and put some colour to his pallid skin. He looked at the network of steep tracks on the slope across the valley. The sight of a lone woman trudging up slowly with a large sack on her back stirred in him a long-forgotten feeling. Over the noise of the car, he could hear the faint jingling of the river far below and the quiet swishing of a thousand trees that thickly layered the uneven mountains.

Earlier they had passed the occasional vehicle, but for the last hour the road had been completely deserted. The driver was beginning to crib audibly, and the sky, a morose grey, rumbled ominously. Google Maps was of no use in this area, but Shekhar sensed that they were approaching his village.

The three small shops along the road were completely dilapidated. Shekhar peered in and called out, even though there was no one in sight. The weary driver began to blow the car horn. Shekhar turned hurriedly to get into the car, feeling sure that the lively marketplace of his village was just a little farther when he stopped short in his tracks. Right in front of him was a towering boulder, its broad rockface tilting slightly onto the road.

It was unmistakable. He turned around in surprise to look at the crumbled shops again, then at the large horse chestnut tree a little ahead. His heart began to race. Unexpectedly and without ceremony, he had arrived.

The driver was reluctant to leave him here in the middle of nowhere, but Shekhar assured him that his village was a short walk down the hillside. Receiving the generous fare, the driver called out several cheerful greetings, but Shekhar was already moving down the dirt path, a small bag in hand, wondering to himself where they had shifted the marketplace.

Recent rain had made the muddy slope slippery, and he walked with cautious steps, while taking in everything around him. The oak and rhododendron trees that shaded the path, rustled softly in response to his gaze. It seemed to him that each stone, each shrub had preserved itself for him, unchanged so that he would be able to recognise his way home. Further down, the terraced fields were overgrown with tall weeds, and the path became a thin parting between the vegetation and sometimes disappeared altogether. They must have made a broader motorable track right up to the village, he thought, which explained the disuse of this path. He was surprised to see how every turn returned to his consciousness like muscle memory, as if he had never been away. Instinctively turning left when the path forked, he remembered himself as a boy running up this slope through fields of mustard. His younger sisters would tag along shouting at him to slow down when he moved too far ahead. Babu, his father, would be loping up the hillside, his thin tall figure clad in a dhoti and coat, late for the morning puja at the temple, of which he was the priest.

Shekhar learnt that going downhill could be as tedious, if not more, as climbing up when the knees had gone city-soft. He sat down on a boulder to rein in both the breathlessness and apprehension he was feeling, one aggravating the other, making his thoughts wander in zigzags just like the trail he was on. Babu ... would he still be alive? He could expect him to be completely unreasonable and unbending in accepting him back.

Getting up and moving down again, he was reminded that mountain paths could be deceptive, destinations that appeared close shifting further as one moved towards them, the gaze not accounting for the numerous upheavals that remained hidden in the folds. Soon he caught sight of the tops of numerous rows of houses, and his nervousness returned. Part of him wanted to turn back and not return to what he had left so long ago. But there was nothing left in the city. He had run huge losses since the pandemic broke out and was forced to sell off his small transport business to pay the bank loans.

The village consisted of several rows of houses, each separated by fields, and now the topmost row was in sight. How would he greet Ija, his mother? She would embrace him dearly, but he would remain unmoved and aloof, he told himself. His sisters would no doubt have married and gone away. But would his baby brother fight with him when he claimed a portion of land where he hoped to rest for some time?

He had expected the village kids to have spotted him from a distance and come running to him, clamouring for city treats, wanting to know his intended destination and running ahead to announce his arrival to the household. He had stuffed his pockets with sweets, remembering the disappointment he had felt as a child when an outsider arrived empty-handed.

He quickened his steps towards the first house in the row, puzzled by the complete silence and apparent disrepair. He moved past it quickly and stood a moment in front of the second house. Holding his breath, he climbed the narrow stone staircase that led into the courtyard. Scattered recollections of a forgotten home reconstructed themselves in the image of what he saw before him. However, the simple stone structure appeared so small, and the sprawling courtyard of his memory was only a few feet wide. But there were no signs of life, and all the doors were locked. Where had they gone? Seized with a sudden desperation, he began to knock on all the doors, calling out loudly for Ija, hoping that one of the windows would fly open and her unaged face would peer out of it. Perhaps they were attending a function somewhere, he thought hopefully, but seeing the state of neglect, he knew that the house had been unoccupied for some time. The neighbours would surely know of their whereabouts, he assured himself. He peered to look down at the other rows of houses, but the overgrown fields impeded his vision. Drained by the long journey, he slumped down onto the parapet to gather his thoughts. His eyes moved over each part of the house, reacquainting himself with it—the worn-out wooden railings, the carved doors and windows stripped of all paint except in a few dark green patches, and the tall grass that had sprouted in between the stone slates of the roof. His eyes finally rested on a courtyard stone, which he expected to see broken and with a small part missing. But he noted that it had been repaired. As Shekhar sat there, forty-four years old, slim but soft around the middle, the chequered beret on his head shading his green-brown eyes, his face lined with numerous regrets, his mouth drawn thin to disguise the feeling of desolation that followed him like a shadow, he remembered himself as the nine-year-old who had left this home.

Being the eldest sibling, he would take care of several chores to make life easier for a fragile Ija. He remembered her as being continuously pregnant. He had learnt to cook at a young age, for on those rare occasions when Ija was menstruating, she was confined to the cowshed. Apart from his three younger siblings, she had delivered two stillborns, and with each birth she became more pinched and frail. Being an upper-caste Brahmin and additionally the temple priest, Babu took pride in creating elaborate rituals at home and would fly into a rage if things were not exactly as he expected. Shekhar would have to wake up early in the morning to recite mantras with him before helping Ija out and rushing to school. Babu had ambitions for Shekhar to become a government officer, and Shekhar had to be very conscientious about schoolwork. Part of his being was devoted towards impressing Babu, and part of it was employed in softening Ija's life. His diligence didn't go unnoticed by Babu but was accepted without a compliment. With every display of sincerity from his son, his expectations only rose. His temper would become aggravated when he found Shekhar faltering on the smallest count.

Shekhar had gone over that particular day in his head several times, tempering the details in his retelling of it to a few trusted friends. But sitting here in that same courtyard by himself, thirty-five years later, he let it come back to him with as much faith as he could repose on his memory. Babu was away to preside over a puja in the neighbouring village. Drinking water needed to be carried to the house from a well about half a kilometre away, and because Ija was not well, Shekhar had excused himself early from school. He was on his second round of ferrying water home when he found Babu sitting in the courtyard, tired from his excursion and scowling fiercely. Realising that his day had not gone well, Shekhar put down the water vessel as quietly as possible and informed him that Ija was ill.

Babu rose and leapt towards him, 'So is that an excuse to miss school?' He grabbed a surprised Shekhar by his collar. 'You want to be tied to your mother's skirts all your life, or do you want to be a man of some worth?'

The humiliation that he had suffered at the puja fuelled his anger and he began beating Shekhar mercilessly. He flung the copper vessel full of water down the slope. Shekhar heard the receding clanging as it rolled down the hillside. Babu grabbed him again and flung him to the ground with all his might. A sharp broken edge of a courtyard stone pierced his right temple. Seeing blood Babu withdrew. Ija rushed out but became paralysed seeing her husband's fury. The baby in her arms had started bawling loudly.

'Get that baby to shut up!' Babu bellowed. Turning to his wounded son he said condescendingly, 'Go get the ghada back, I'll prepare a patti,' and went in.

Shekhar rose from the ground, pressing his bleeding temple, gulping down his sobs and shame and under the shocked watching eyes of Ija and the neighbours, he left the house, ostensibly to retrieve the water vessel. But that display of arbitrary and unreasonable savagery had in a moment snapped that cord of reverence that tied Shekhar devotedly to Babu. As he walked down the village path listening to whispered commiserations from neighbours, he wanted, with the same earnestness that he had earlier sought his father's approval, to hurt him grievously.

The years that followed were a blur. His first few stops were in towns not far from his village, cleaning tables at roadside dhabas. At that time the distance had seemed immense and, not wanting to risk being found, he changed his surname. When his anger subsided, it was shame and fear that kept him from coming back. As he had struggled in the world for the last thirty-five years, moving up slowly, being in a big city and in a failed marriage, his village had become the vision of all that he had missed in life. Had they looked for him at all? Did his father regret his actions? Had his mother been able to protect the younger children? These unresolved questions had haunted him all these years and kept him tied to a childhood that he had lost too early. Years later he had reverted to his original surname, partly as an attempt to establish a connection with his past and partly, to claim his elevated caste status in society. The thought of returning had come to him several times, but with the passing of years his courage had faded.

As the monsoon evening fell on the valley, a dense fog arose from its depths, creeping silently like a demon into the courtyard, wrapping the house in a layer of mist, preparing to confound this man who thought he had found his home. Shekhar pulled himself together to seek the neighbours when his eye fell above the doorway. He was reminded that an image of Lord Shiva used to be embossed there but it was missing now. Perhaps he had walked into the wrong courtyard! Feeling hopeful once more, he quickly ran down the dirt path but was dismayed to find the next house also deserted and in a greater state of disrepair. His used to be the second … no third house, wasn't it? Maybe more houses had come up after he left, he thought.

As Shekhar moved from one row of houses to another, past the fields that separated them, the mist rushed towards him riding on a strong gust of wind from the valley below, silently erasing the village from his view and adding to his confusion. Every house in the village was built in more or less the same fashion and each presented some anomalies from his memory of the home he had occupied so long ago.

He could barely see the path in front of him and with every step forward, the homecoming that he had been thinking about for years was moving away from him. He beat down the nettles that blocked the path to the last row of houses. As he groped his way down to the edge of the village, he realised that it was entirely deserted.

The thick mist hung absolutely still now and with night descending, its pure whiteness sullied into a dull grey. The rising sound of the cicadas pierced through its seemingly impenetrable shroud, pronouncing the silence of the entire valley. His legs quivered with exhaustion and his heart was limp with profound disappointment.

He began to move back to retrieve his bag, taking one tentative step at a time, not wanting to risk a fall down the slope, when a sudden gust of wind cleared the fog around him and a dark doorway revealed itself to him. He peered at it in the fading light. His throat constricted as his eyes fell on a carving of Lord Shiva above the doorway. He had found it! How had he missed it before? The wooden door gently beckoned him into the warmth of its fold.

He decided it would be safer to retrieve his luggage in the morning. The rusted padlock on the main door gave way after a few hard pulls. The door creaked softly as he pushed it open. He got onto the other side quickly, shutting out the devilish fog with relief and stood in total darkness. Switching on the torch on his mobile phone, he climbed the narrow mud-coated staircase that led to the rooms above the cowshed. The room on the right of the staircase used to be his father's puja room but was now bare. He peered at a frayed calendar on the wall with a large familiar image of goddess Laxmi smiling benignly. The date read July, 2013. That was the year floods had devastated the hills and probably the year his family had moved away. Where had they gone? What had they done with the goats and cows? he wondered as he moved through the rest of the house.

The house had a dusty and stale smell, however the indescribable feeling of finally being home was sufficient comfort for his exhausted body. He inspected every bare nook and corner, a calming warmth spreading inside him. Finally he came to the room he used to sleep in, keeping that for the last to savour at length. He collapsed onto a bare coir cot which sagged under his weight, its rough cords biting into his skin. He was terribly cold and looking for some kind of cover he found an old sheet and a pillow in a corner of the room. He had to curl his body as tightly as possible to keep himself from shivering.

It began to rain hard. The water hit the stone-tiled roof like metal pellets but was unable to drown a doleful wailing sound that was unsettling him. He listened to it intently. It sounded like a woman in mourning. He thought of Ija wistfully. His lasting memory of her was her face transfixed with fear and her body completely subdued into inaction on the day he left home. Over the years the extreme guilt that he felt towards her, the deep suffering he knew he had no doubt caused her, and his inability to do anything about it, had transformed into a resentment which became more overpowering than the anger that he felt towards his father. However, deep down he had been sure that she would still be waiting for him.

He dug his face into the pillow which, though musty, brought back to him her smell—a mixture of soap and grass—a smell that he often woke up to all through these long years. Unlike Babu, Ija had always been effusive in her display of love for him. When Shekhar grazed the goats in the pastures near the forest she would slip away from home with treats from the kitchen hidden in the folds of her ghaghra. Amidst the muted shuffling of the short green grass she would hug him dearly to her breast. On rainy nights like these she would sit patting him to sleep, her face weary with the unending burden that life had apportioned to her, her fair skin worn-out to a permanent jaundiced pallor. And now the thought of her made him want to go out and soothe that dramatic wailing that the mischievous wind had conjured.

The cheerful and raucous twittering of birds outside belied the cold dark gloom of the room that Shekhar woke up in. It took him a long moment to remember where he was. The pillow that he had hugged to himself all night was caked with stale brown residue. He threw it away, repelled by its sharp odour, surprised that it had smelt different in the dark of the night. Sunlight had crept into the room through the cracks in the wooden windowpanes and, filtered by dense cobwebs, it cast a dim pattern on a framed photograph on the wall. Stiff with cold, Shekhar got up with difficulty from the sagging bed and took the frame off the hook that it hung precariously from. It was covered with a sticky layer of dirt.

He dragged himself out into the golden warmth that had filled the pale-coloured stone courtyard. As he sat on the low broad parapet his limbs began to thaw immediately, and eager to get a glimpse of his family, he pulled out the photograph from its cracked frame. He looked at it for a long time. An unknown family stared back at him. As he looked up he experienced an illusion of the mountains across receding from him. He steadied himself, holding onto the parapet to keep from falling off. He threw away the photograph. He turned to look bitterly at the house which became a stranger to him in an instant.

Everything was still except for thin sheets of clouds that swept swiftly across the sky. He had heard of entire villages getting deserted in the Uttarakhand hills by villagers desperate for job opportunities and easier lives, but had never in his wildest imagination thought that his would be one of those ghost villages.

His stomach protested with a loud grumble and he was reminded that he hadn't eaten since the previous afternoon. Was it only yesterday that he had arrived? It seemed like a long time ago.

His bag lay in the open in the courtyard he had left it in, completely soaked. He opened a packet of biscuits and hungrily went through it. Feeling a little sick after that, he threw up. He had no drinking water so he glugged down half a bottle of juice. He decided to go to the school that was high up on the ridge to his left, hoping to find someone there or on the main road that went past it. As he moved through the eerie silence of deserted rows of houses he was disconcerted by small details—a bamboo basket lying in a doorway, a rusted sickle hanging outside a window, a faded scrap of a sari clipped onto a clothesline—it seemed as if any moment people might emerge from inside and have a late start to this day.

Several thoughts swirled in his head as he trudged up. How should he go back when he had no money left? How should he locate his family? The land was there for his taking but was that all he wanted? How would he prove to the next person who came along that this was his land? What had he hoped to find here? What had he ...? Feeling jumpy and agitated he fumbled and slipped several times and took many wrong turns.

Stopping for a breather he spotted some houses on the mountain across the valley. He looked keenly for some signs of life but they too seemed deserted. He remembered that the village was Tallagaon, where craftsmen lived. Considered to be of a lower caste, they were separated clearly from the higher castes, who lived in Mallagaon, Shekhar's village, by a considerable physical distance, to avoid any unnecessary contact. Babu would not let even their shadow fall on him and purified himself whenever their paths crossed.

Resuming the hard climb, he finally arrived at a clearing, completely exhausted. The school building was in ruins. Broken down mercilessly. The forest had taken over, throwing curly vines across dilapidated walls, sprouting seedlings of trees where once children had sat on cold cement floors poring over books. He waded through the wet vegetation thinking of the endless hours he had spent, even in the short span of his life here, diligently parroting teachers.

He found a small classroom which was somewhat intact. The floor was littered with soiled books and broken desks as if a sudden storm had swept everyone away. He walked around the room, hoping to find maybe a phone number scrawled on a notebook, or some clue to help him to proceed from here. He spotted a chart which hung askew on a wall, no doubt the handiwork of a young enthusiastic teacher. It mapped the migration of people into the Uttarakhand Himalayas over the centuries. While Babu would claim that they had lived in this land forever, Shekhar remembered Ija telling him of how they had come from so many parts of the Indian subcontinent, seeking a safe haven from persecution, humiliation, defeat and sometimes in search of opportunities, land and even God. In the generous embrace of the mountains, they forged their identities but only to differentiate again. Ruing at the pointlessness of an education that separated them from their land, that crushed the dignity of the weak, and which could not keep the children safe, Shekhar gulped down the sour taste he still had in his mouth from retching in the morning. He looked with despair at the torn charts that lay scattered on the floor, formulas and alphabets, failing to assemble into any meaning.

Outside, he sat looking at the mountains decreasing in degrees of saturation as they receded into a blurry pale blue infinity, the plains from where he himself had returned and where all the people of his village had gone, to merge with the unknown multitudes. He continued to stare blankly ahead, there was no course of action to deliberate on, all roads had come to a dead-end.

As the day wore on, the mist began to rise again from deep down in the valley. Looking for something to anchor his thoughts, Shekhar watched it rise in a hypnotic upward swirl, gently erasing everything in its path, when his eyes fell on a tendril of smoke rising from one of the houses in Tallagaon. Goggling his eyes with his hands he discerned a dot of movement in one of the courtyards, like a sweep of dark skirts.

Feverish with excitement he was racing down the path the next moment. There was still time to make the long walk to the other side before dark. The woman would definitely have an address or phone number of someone from his village, he thought as he doubled his speed. The path plunged straight down to the riverbed, not rising and falling as most mountain paths do, as if making up for the numerous disappointments that had been heaped upon him in quick succession.

He stumbled across the shallow stream which was lined with long ferns. Undisturbed by humans, thick moss had spread itself out lavishly on the boulders along it, making the walk slippery.

As he started working his way up towards Tallagaon, he came into the fold of the mist and had to concentrate on every step he took. When he reached the edge of the village he noticed a stack of handwoven bamboo baskets lying neglected in the corner of a courtyard. Here too a sense of desolation hung in the air. Shekhar tried unsuccessfully to recall the name of the boy from this village who was in his class and who he had been instructed to discreetly avoid in school.

He moved desperately from one locked door to another, through the mist that was thickening around him rapidly. Had he imagined that vision of a woman? His progress came to a complete halt as everything around him disappeared from sight. He looked down to see the foggy remnants of his own body, and in a blink he was completely swallowed by the encasing greyness. He stood still listening to his breathing. It was as if only his thoughts existed, and all that he had ever been was erased in that moment.

It was hard for him to guess how long he stood there before he heard the soft tinkling of a bell. The image of a shrine came to his mind, a small one inside a house, illuminated by a robust wick, orange light falling on little pictures of deities, his mother's tall back bowing down to them. He was not bound by faith to this vision, but by the memory of warmth and security it had evoked so long ago. If it is possible to feel deep sadness and a sense of complete fulfilment at the same time, that is what Shekhar experienced at that moment. A strong gust of wind dissipated the fog and the world around him reappeared. Right in front of him was a large patch of marigolds. He caught a whiff of prasad being roasted in pure ghee. He turned around to see a short old lady moving towards him, wrapped in a black ghagra and stole.

'Lalit, you are back?' she cried with joy. 'I knew you would be back soon.' She reached to take his face in her rough hands, her cataract-ridden eyes peering out of her dark, wrinkled face. 'I have waited for you.'

He bent towards her, deciding to be what she wanted him to be. As she crushed him to her breast, he smelled soap, grass and, yes, marigolds.

The next morning she gave him a handful of seeds. The monsoon was upon them, and they had not yet sown the crop for autumn. He walked past the fruit grove to get to the fields. The snake that was sunning itself under the kaku tree gently slithered away. Shekhar plucked a kaku that was half eaten by birds and bit into it. As he tilled the land, Ija cooked the afternoon meal.

Crazy Love

The village to which no motorable road led, and that was plunged so deep into the narrow valley that the sun rose late and set very early, was aptly named Anyargaon, the dark village. Winter, when shadows ate up most of the day, was brutal and strained even the strongest of spirits. And she, whose dark form stood against the sky, was stained by years of despair. As a bitter wind swept through the valley, it set the slopes into gentle waves, and the sound of the splashing treetops was like a distant sea. Her blue ghaghra flapped sharply in the wind. She shivered violently, moving her gaze away from the bald peak where a lone deformed tree stabbed the deep blue above it. The glistening river at her feet flowed down ceaselessly, almost noiselessly, pooling in a recess under a rocky overhang, and here untouched by sunlight it seemed to have soaked up eons of darkness into its inky depths. He slept inside, warm and safe, and blessing him with the memory of the sunny slopes of her own childhood, she stepped into the pool, immersing herself in the darkness that had crept into her mind.

All through his childhood, Trilok was given the moniker 'jhaant', meaning a troublemaker, by the villagers—he fought to claim the heaviest log when a tree fell and the wood was distributed amongst the villagers, ate the biggest meal at a feast, and teased every old amma to a fit of irritation. His mother laughed at his exploits, hoping that her uncensored love for her only son would protect him from the despondency that was taking an increasing hold of her. When she disappeared, Trilok, who was only thirteen then, led the search party for three nights and days. Her body was found washed up on the riverbank a few kilometres down their village. It was he who spotted her bright blue ghaghra between the reeds. He rushed towards her but stopped short of touching her. As they turned the body on its back, he walked away. He did not speak or eat for two days. After that he behaved like nothing had happened. He never spoke of her again and brushed off sympathy with a snigger. But his childish brashness was gone with her.

Even after his wife's death and his son Trilok's sudden transformation, Pratap Singh could not be persuaded to move away from Anyargaon. No one in the village knew when and why their ancestors had come to settle in this cold valley. And now most of its inhabitants were gone, one by one—it was better to be in a small patch of sunlight wherever that might be—and only five families remained. But despite the barren slopes, the land itself was made fertile by the river, and the few who had stayed back for lack of better prospects had large tracts to cultivate and plenty of produce to sell.

Gayatri was accompanying Aiee, her mother, to the ration shop in the marketplace when Pratap Singh saw her. He had stopped for tea before resuming the long walk to Anyargaon, which was on the other side of the mountain. Gayatri was sixteen. Her face was gently framed with wavy hair, giving her, in the eyes of Pratap, a simple yet alluring beauty. All his daughters had married and gone away, and now getting his only son Trilok married would ensure that the house would be looked after as it should.

He followed Gayatri and her mother home and put forward his proposal. Aiee was offended when she learnt where he was from—how could she send her daughter off to that godforsaken place? But Babu, Gayatri's father, argued that Pratap owned a lot of land, which Trilok could sell and move out of the village. But most importantly, Pratap was asking for no dowry. Babu had inherited land, which they lived off, but he had no income to put together a dowry for his only daughter, and the thought of getting her married had been worrying him for some time.

In her childhood, Gayatri had been the envy of every little girl in the village, pampered by her father, who carried her on his shoulders everywhere he went. She was allowed to cut her hair short and wear skirts in a time when other young girls wore saris. The girls teased her that her father would definitely find her a groom who lived in the city, that being the measure of a father's love. But the slip from the most-favoured child to her mother's assistant had been a quick one as soon as she turned nine or ten. While her brothers helped out in the fields, they did no chores inside the house. Gayatri had to discontinue school on her mother's orders. She had hoped that Babu would fight against the decision, but discovered that since she was no longer a cherubic child, she was no longer entitled to special treatment. And now she listened with trepidation as Babu argued in favour of the proposal. Gayatri had heard of Anyargaon, a forgotten village tucked away at the bottom of a rocky valley. For once in his life, Babu had his way, and the date was fixed for the upcoming wedding season.

Trilok saw Gayatri in her village marketplace a few days before their wedding. He would not have noticed her otherwise, but now that he did he was instantly attracted to the calm, reassuring air she had about her. And Gayatri saw him too—the sun in his eyes and in his hair. She froze when she realised that he was trying to exchange looks with her, and when he made as if to move towards her she ran away nervously. Rounding the corner, she was leaning against a wall, flustered, settling her hair and ruing her appearance, when he appeared right in front of her. They looked at each other for a long breathless moment before Gayatri turned her head away awkwardly and he broke into a bashful smile.

'Shall I drop you home?' he asked, looking at the large heavy sack that she was carrying.

She shook her head and began racing down the slope, stopping to look back only when she had moved away a considerable distance. He was still standing and watching her. At that safe distance from him, she broke into a fit of giggles and didn't stop till she reached home. And that image—when his handsome face broke into a smile and his light brown eyes held her gaze—she carried with her forever. It erased the anxiety of going to Anyargaon and she felt reassured that he would always be there to protect her.

Trilok too had a lightness in his step that day as he walked back home through the forest. He looked at the sun moving along with him, and his smile in that moment carried no trace of the shadows that lurked within.

Aiee sensed a change in Gayatri's mood and commented that it was not decent for her to be humming and singing to herself all day, to seem so eager to be married. Aiee herself was increasingly troubled in the lead-up to the wedding, and Gayatri would often have to bear the brunt of her irritable mood. She participated in the wedding ceremony sullenly, and at the time of the bidai, when the newlyweds were touching her feet, she grabbed Gayatri by her arm and announced that she was too young to be sent off to her sasuraal yet and that Pratap Singh could send for her after a few months. Needless to say, everyone was bewildered and tried to argue her out of it, but she began to sob helplessly and remained adamant. Since underage marriages had begun to be frowned upon of late, Pratap thought it best to keep quiet. Gayatri, who had begun to cry at the thought of leaving her parents' home, now cried for an entirely different reason. Babu knew that opposing his wife would mean an ugly scene in front of the guests, so he merely consoled Gayatri, telling her that Aiee's love was making her protective and that it would be best to wait for some time. Everyone agreed with him—perhaps Aiee had lost the courage to send off her daughter to that doomed valley.

When the guests had left, Gayatri sat in her room looking out into the empty courtyard where glittering streamers fluttered silently in the wind. Aiee and Babu argued bitterly. Why had she agreed to the match in the first place if this is what she had in mind? He spoke in a thin, high-pitched voice, which had become shriller in his bafflement. He had twisted her arm into agreeing, she retorted. Gayatri's brothers also weighed in with their objections to their mother's decision. Feeling cornered, Aiee lashed out at them with the real reason behind her decision.

'How will I take care of the enormous load of work by myself if she goes away? Now that you boys have moved away, even the work in the fields has to be done by Gayatri and me,' she cried out.

'It would be better to sell those fields, put the money in a postal account for the boys, and send the girl off with her husband,' Babu argued.

Aiee was screaming in rage now. 'I will *not* sell a foot of land that belongs to my sons! In a year or two, Mahesh will get married, and I will have a helping hand. Gayatri will be free to go then.'

She did have a point, the boys agreed; it was true that Aiee could not manage everything by herself. Babu kept muttering his objections, but Aiee shut him up by pointing out that the groom and his family had accepted her decision, so why couldn't he? Babu knew that her opinion was so strong that it was impossible to counter it. The matter was settled. Gayatri shut her window and went off to sleep.

As the months went by, Trilok became more and more withdrawn and began spending most of his time in the forest. Amidst the tall trees, which stood erect on the almost vertical inclines, seemingly defying gravity, the voices of neighbours (who spoke of him as one followed by a tenacious shadow of ill-fate) faded away. The village was far below, along the river that was flung across the length of the narrow valley. For Trilok, this space had signified the absence of his mother, and now that feeling had intensified. He remembered the bitter quarrels between his parents, when his mother would urge his father to leave the village, begging him to pay attention to the intense fear that was growing inside her. But Pratap was always dismissive and chided her for having such a pessimistic view of life.

A year passed with no word from Gayatri's family. Pratap tried to persuade Trilok to annul the marriage or plan an elopement. Trilok made no response. Pratap ignored his relatives' advice of leaving the village for his son's sake, and decided instead to send him away for a while, to the nearest town.

Even though this town was only a hundred kilometres away from Anyargaon, Trilok felt he had travelled a long way. On the night he arrived, he looked at the hillsides that twinkled like a night-sky fallen on earth, shivering with an aliveness that he had never felt before, lying awake till time faded into a dusty morning.

He took in the crowds and bazaars with the simple wonder of a young man who had spent the first twenty-two years of his life in a wilderness. It was not that he was here for some grand purpose but merely to study in the government college. A distant relative, who had witnessed the embarrassment of his wedding, agreed to host him for some time.

For Alka, who had also moved there recently, the town was a disappointment. It once had glory, she had heard, but now it seemed like a painting gone wrong—house upon house strung in rows over hillsides, like gaudy painted lanterns stuck clumsily by a child on a large piece of brown-coloured paper. She wondered why this town existed at all. Like many small towns, it seemed merely a portal to the city, with its inhabitants looking for opportunities for themselves or their children to step out of its sterility. When her father decided to move back to the hills from a bustling city, she had a notion that it would be to a village at the foot of white mountains. It was true that you could see the Himalayas from the town on a clear day, but they were far, far away.

His sunny good looks made Trilok instantly popular in college, a stage in life when girls did not pay much attention to money and prospects. He never spoke of his circumstances, and being a little older than the rest of his classmates, he had a certain 'older brother' quality that drew even the boys to him. Alka was instantly attracted to him and, when she learnt that he came from a small village, she felt she had found the love of her life.

He was drawn to her too—she belonged to a world that he wanted to move towards—yet he held back, keeping himself carefully out of reach. But Alka pursued him relentlessly, his reticence making him even more desirable. She often turned up at his relative's house with home-cooked food, spending Sunday afternoons with them, enjoying being the centre of attention. To Trilok's rustic relatives, her city manners and frankness made her utterly charming, and they took care not to mention Trilok's marriage in her presence.

Her romantic notions of village life were so naïve that it made Trilok laugh, even as they softened his own feelings towards it. It was difficult to not respond to her, and slowly he began to resent Gayatri for the pickle she had put his life into.

Alka insisted on travelling with him to Anyargaon during a short break in college. Trilok was hesitant but didn't quite know how to refuse her. He made sure to hurry past Gayatri's village. While the villagers were shocked with the forwardness of this unmarried couple travelling together, Pratap himself was relieved to see that Trilok had moved on. Alka's unabashed enthusiasm for rustic peculiarities and exaggerated displays of affection for everyone she met—whether human or animal—were amusing and endearing. It was a happy time for Trilok in Anyargaon.

Back in town, he opened himself completely to Alka's affections. One Sunday afternoon when they were together, a young boy came asking for him and led him to the main street in the crowded bazaar. Trilok's heart lurched when he saw Gayatri standing on the sidewalk, looking very much like the villager she was. He moved towards her with mixed feelings. She told him that she was there to attend a friend's wedding. They stood awkwardly on the side of the busy road, complete strangers to each other. But the sight of her demure form and the hopeful eyes that she looked at him with evoked a strong sympathetic passion in Trilok.

She could not hold back the tears at the moment of parting. He made a promise to send word for her on his next trip to the village.

When Alka learned the truth, she was completely heartbroken. After the initial shock had passed, she tried to persuade Trilok to get a divorce, but failing to convince him, she stopped coming to college altogether. Trilok hadn't expected such an extreme reaction and suffered to have hurt Alka so much, the one person who had made Anyargaon bearable for him.

For Gayatri, whose days and months had been filled with anticipation intertwined with infinite waiting, Anyargaon, a home she had never seen, had become a promise of better days. But because she was unsure of Trilok's feelings for her, she hesitated to assert herself too much. A few months ago, Babu had been killed in an accident on his way back from a wedding—the drunken bus driver had gone over the edge on a sharp turn, hurtled down a steep hillside, and plunged into a river. They were lucky to find his body, as most were swept away in the river. Gayatri mourned for him deeply, still able to feel his warm skin in the hollow behind her knees, remembering her childhood when she had gazed down at the world from atop his shoulders. She had hoped that Trilok and his father would come to commiserate and that she would insist on leaving with them, but that never happened. She had also heard that failing to persuade Trilok to get married again, Pratap had got a young bride for himself, and Gayatri was not sure if she would be welcome in their home anymore. But when she heard about a woman friend accompanying Trilok to his village, an alarmed Gayatri took the opportunity of a friend's wedding in a neighbouring village and slipped away to meet him. She had rehearsed her lines, how she would reprimand him, tell him that she would wait for him forever, and as soon as her circumstances allowed, run away to be with him. But as they stood awkwardly on the sidewalk, she noticed the change in his looks—a certain refinement that the town had given him—and became nervous, conscious of her own shiny clothes and the fact that she was not wearing sindoor (which she had worn in the early days after her marriage till Aiee put a stop to it). When he promised to send word for her on his next trip to the village, she felt completely reassured, like the first time she had laid eyes on him.

Aiee sensed her restlessness. In response to relatives who had begun to weigh in on Gayatri's behalf, urging her to be reasonable and compassionate towards her only daughter, she would taunt her to be off and gone if she liked. Then, as if determined, to hold onto Gayatri as the keeper of her brothers' property and as her own caretaker, she had a stroke which paralysed one half of her body. Gayatri knew that her fate was sealed.

Trilok did send word for her on his next visit to Anyargaon and waited in the forest an entire day. A day that was full of emotions that he could not name—it was neither joy nor apprehension he felt but a certain calm that lingered around him, ready to step into him at the sight of Gayatri. But she didn't come. As he walked home in the darkness, a familiar heartsickness took over again. It was the next day that he heard of her mother's condition and realised that the possibility of them being together was gone forever. He returned to town, but it was no longer the same. Alka was gone.

In the next few years Trilok vacillated between despondency and industry, avoiding going to Anyargaon altogether. Always restless, he would either wander around town aimlessly or would lock himself up in his room for several days. Nothing could hold his attention for long, and after studying law for two years he decided to drop out. He spent most of the money that Pratap sent on alcohol. He invested in a hotel after taking a big loan from Pratap, but it was a doomed project. Pratap, who in turn had taken the loan from his daughters' husbands, had to write off most of his property to them. His young wife was so distressed that she left for her parents' home with their son, vowing never to return to the desolate hell.

It wasn't long before Trilok was forced to return to Anyargaon. He had no means to survive in town. The village wrecked him completely. The shadows began to extend into his mind, the silence, broken only by the sinister rush of the river, was oppressive, and the towering dark mountains intensified his feelings of insignificance. He became hostile towards Pratap, seeing him as the main culprit in the tragedy of his life, even accusing him of killing his mother. When he started becoming a menace, he was once again given the childhood nickname of 'jhaant', the mischief-maker. His mood swings, like his mother's, resulted in angry outbursts, but Pratap refused to accept that he needed medical help. In all this time Trilok never once mentioned Gayatri.

The years had not passed without making their impression on Gayatri. Each harvest, tending to her brothers' fields in the harsh sun, was marked by deep furrows on her forehead. All her brothers were married and settled in cities and towns, and none of their wives wanted to stay back in the village. Gayatri took care that Aiee did not have a single bedsore despite her increasing disability. When the brothers took away several sacks of grains on their yearly visits, there was still some produce left to sell in the local shop. This gave Gayatri an income to run the house, apart from the small sums that the brothers left for Aiee's treatment. She would hear about Trilok now and then—about his business venture having failed and about him being back in the village and 'creating trouble' for everyone. She had, after her last meeting with Trilok, started wearing sindoor again, defiantly drawing a thick line of red powder in the parting of her hair, which would smear onto her forehead by the end of the day. The yearning she had for Trilok had slipped into her essence, and the comfort of a shared fate bound her to him irrevocably.

One winter afternoon, after Gayatri had given Aiee an oil massage in the sun, she busied herself with pounding soaked rice into chewda. With all the weight of her body, she thumped a thick log into a hole in the courtyard. Just as she paused for a breather, she heard a muffled scream. She spun around and caught a glimpse of a snake's tail disappearing into a shrub near Aiee. Gayatri froze. In those few seconds she reimagined her life. Perhaps it was possible. Perhaps, for the first time in her life, she could make a decision for herself. As she saw Aiee's body convulsing, she hesitated. Should she call the neighbours or should she run in and get a patti to tie above the bite?

But her feet felt rooted to the ground. The poison spread quickly through Aiee's body.

As she lay in the courtyard with the local vaid medicating her and an old lady performing 'jhaad phoonk' Aiee held Gayatri's arm in a tight grip, her fearful eyes looking at her accusingly even as she struggled tenaciously to hang onto her vegetable-like existence. Finally her hold loosened. When Gayatri watched Aiee's body go up in flames, she felt a deeper kinship with her than she had when she was alive, as if she could never separate her from her own being. What followed was an immense emptiness, not relief.

There would be a time, much later, when women would have their share of the inheritence, but that time had not yet come, and Gayatri, continuing to care for the household as before, silently witnessed minor arguments as the property was divided amongst the brothers. It was decided that they would not sell the land and Gayatri would keep taking care of the fields in lieu of staying in the house. They needed the yearly relief from the summer heat of the plains.

Two weeks after Aiee's death, Gayatri got up very early in the morning and made khajur—a sweetmeat made with flour and sugar syrup and fried to just the right brownness. She packed some in a piece of clean cloth, making sure to leave enough for her brothers. She tied her belongings in an old sari and, placing the bundle on her head, began her walk to Anyargaon, not stopping even once to look at the fields and the house that she had tended with so much care all these years.

It was a long walk, but she only stopped once, before the final descent into the village. After a short rest she braced herself for what lay ahead. The slope got steeper, and scattered in the quiet darkness of the groves lay mounds of half-melted snow. The air was sharp and clean and stung with every breath.

Anyargaon was at the bottom of the slope. Houses were flung far and wide on the stony banks of the river that cut across the valley. Pratap Singh was working in the fields when Gayatri arrived. She had expected hostility and resistance and was determined to brave it all, but instead there was tremendous relief on Pratap's face when he recognised her. She saw that his stern and upright countenance was broken completely. He, in turn, smiled ruefully at the woman in front of him, aged so much beyond her years, remembering the pretty girl he had chosen for his only son all those years ago.

Gayatri's heart beat rapidly, and her restless eyes looked for Trilok. As they moved towards the house, she began to hear faint shouts and thumps. Pratap paused a moment near the door of the cowshed. A chill slipped down Gayatri's spine as he swung the door open. Trilok was tied with thick ropes to wooden pegs meant for cows. His hair was long and matted, and his once strong body had shrunk to skin and bones. Now she understood that this is what the talk of Trilok's 'creating trouble' had really meant.

Seeing a stranger in front of him, Trilok quietened down and began apologising for the mess, begging her to convince 'this man' to untie him. Gayatri clutched at the creaking door, looking at the man she had pined for all these years, in the home that she had dreamt of every night.

Pratap pulled her away from that darkness and sat her down on the staircase. A cold wind whined around the fields. As the shock died down, Gayatri rested in the comfort of the sun-warmed stones. She looked at the steep dark slopes and at that bird that flew against the sunlight, so high above it all. After a few minutes, Pratap spoke, his eyes filled with regret. 'It is this village. Nothing good can come of staying here.' He sighed. 'Perhaps it would be better for you to go back home,' he added quietly.

'I am home,' Gayatri replied without looking at him.

She unpacked her clothes in the room above the cowshed, listening to a fresh bout of abuses from below, preparing herself for the life she had to live out now. She would take care of Trilok as she had taken care of her mother. She tried to convince Pratap to untie him, but he would not hear of it, he couldn't lose Trilok like he had lost his wife.

Gayatri looked after Trilok diligently for some months. He would not allow her to clean him or the shed, kicking hard with his free leg and abusing her if she went near him. She could only go in when he was asleep or held down by Pratap. When the violent outbursts died down, he would be apologetic. Her sleep was always disturbed by his sporadic ranting and thumping through the night. She could see in his eyes that he wanted to end it all, that he was irreparably damaged by the darkness within him. With every passing day in that bitter winter, she realised that for her love for him to live on, he would have to go.

She nudged open the door of the cowshed. Moonlight swept in, littering the floor with dried leaves and dust.

He lay asleep on a bundle of hay. She groped around in the darkness and began to pry open the heavy knot on the thick dirty rope that tied his foot to a wooden peg. She struggled silently, but when she looked up, she saw the stark whites of his eyes in the darkness. She timidly withdrew to sit against the wall, not wanting to set off the screams, which would wake up Pratap. The eyes followed her. She held her breath and looked at the fissured mud-caked wall that looked like parched cracked earth. An ant disappeared into a crack. She could hear the faraway rhythmic clattering of logs that were stuck in a dark recess in the river.

Trilok began talking distractedly; the distinction between dreams and reality blurred. Gayatri sat listening to him, for the first time privy to the inner world that spun in his head and that he was the sum total of. He had brought back his mother from the dead, and she waited for him upstairs. His hotel was flourishing, and he was thinking of opening one in the village. Alka would be happy to stay there, right at the foot of the snow-capped mountains. That golden pin that he had stolen from Minu Amma, and which she had kept looking for till she died, was hidden under his bed. And Gayatri ... she spun towards him, hearing her name for the first time in all these months ... but he had gone silent.

She waited for him to fall asleep before continuing to untie the knots. She left the door ajar and went up to her room. Lying in bed, she listened intently. It was a couple of hours before she heard the loud thud of the cowshed door. She peered out of her window and saw his silhouette hurtling towards the fields below, away from the wretched life his father was determined to tie him to. She imagined the unseen eyes that waited in the dark forest, the hungry swirls under the satin surface of the water, and the lingering icy embrace of the night and knew that death would be swift.

Three days later they found his body a few kilometres down on the riverbed. Gayatri washed off her red sindoor in the same inky waters that had set Trilok free. She slept deeply that night in the undisturbed silence.

The lengthy omnipresent shadows in Anyargaon did not haunt Gayatri; instead they gave her cover from the harshness of the sun when she tilled the fields she owned, next to the house that was hers. Spring offered patches of colour to make up for the desolation of winter, and the empty summer was followed by replenishing rains. Clinging to the craggy slopes were giant beehives that dripped honey—someday she might venture to collect some. Where the river pooled in a dark recess, brightly coloured fish glided just below the surface, and she caught them in her palms as she swam with them.

In the long life that she would live, Gayatri often looked up at that lone bare tree, atop the bald mountain. She would imagine that it was Trilok looking down at her, smiling as he had on that first day.

Where the Road Ends

Gulab's tall, lean body melted into the solid stillness of the grassy slope that he lay on, while his mind floated up towards the eagle gliding in the clear blue summer sky, vanishing into the sun and then appearing again, leaving in its flight a trail of bright spots. His head was light, and the end of the roll was still between his fingers. The occasional bleats of the sheep resting in the shade blended into the murmurs of this bugyal above the treeline. Far below, lonesome village houses gazed down at soundless rivers that cut rough paths deep in the valley. To his left, several mountain ridges ran off in different directions, and to his right, muddied glaciers melted into slim, serpentine streams. And above the glaciers rose the magnificent Himalayas, their whiteness stained by large black patches due to poor snowfall this year.

The sound that made him snap out of his reverie was like a distant gunshot, followed by a low, sustained rumble. He felt a mild tremor in the earth he lay on. He raised himself with some difficulty as the weight returned to his body and looked at the valley below. A wisp of cloud had wandered into his line of vision and stood like a ghost before being swept away by a gust of wind. Even from this distance he could see the bare slope that had been blasted away to make way for the motorable road that was slowly creeping up to the village below.

The sudden flight of an unseen bird drew his attention to a figure moving up towards him. It wasn't the gait of a trekker, more that of a local mountain person. He was hurrying up the slope with his hands clasped behind him, as if he had some urgent news to convey. But Gulab had no ties with anyone in the world, and what could anyone possibly have to tell him that was of any urgency? Unless there was someone terribly sick in the village and they needed jadi-booti from him. He turned his eyes again to the motorable road, an uneasiness settling into him.

Even though he did not participate in the machinations of progress that the humanity below him were engaged in, silent changes had crept into the wilderness around him too. Glaciers had shrunk rapidly in the last twenty years, and the pattern of rains had become unpredictable, causing landslides and floods even high up in the mountains.

Strangely, the man who had been in such a rush until now slowed down as he neared Gulab and, without greeting him, sat down a few metres away. He began to casually pluck grass and shred it to bits while casting furtive glances in Gulab's direction. Gulab, in his turn, observed him with a direct gaze. Of lean build and medium height, he seemed to be in his mid-thirties, was balding early, had sunburnt shiny skin and narrow, shifty eyes. He was wearing army fatigues and boots. Seeing him make no movement towards conversation, Gulab got up, dusted off grass from his handmade sheep-wool coat and trousers and went into his shelter. It was a largish enclosure, covered with hay and sheets of plastic, his home when he came to the high-altitude pastures for summer with his sheep.

When Gulab emerged with a tin mug full of black tea, the man was lingering outside the shelter. It was Gulab's custom to serve refreshments to the rare passer-by, a trekker or a local looking for keeda jadi—wild strawberries, cooked wild mushrooms or biscuits if his supplies were recently replenished from the village below. But today he had only tea to offer to this stranger. The man accepted it with exaggerated gratitude—folded his hands and touched them to his forehead—and broke into a wide smile, revealing a large and perfectly aligned set of bright white teeth.

'You didn't recognise me, Gulab Bhinjiu? I'm Kishan from Halbunia village.'

Gulab betrayed a flicker of emotion at the mention of the village.

'Your son's cousin brother.' His voice was raspy and low, and Shera, the older of the Bhotia sheepdogs, came out of the shelter and began growling at the stranger.

Gulab looked at him squarely before withdrawing and going up the slope to check on his sheep. Clouds were beginning to gather, and like most evenings in these climes, there would be a downpour.

'His mother's brother's son.' Not having got an expected response, Kishan continued to clarify, his eyes gleaming with sly provocation as he followed Gulab at a safe distance. 'Your wife's nephew. I was born after you left her, but I know you very well.'

Shera was sniffing him, his tail tucked between his hind legs, his rusted spiked collar touching his leg. Kishan looked anxiously at his big black hairy body and became absolutely still, afraid that he might jump at his throat. Soon, to his relief, the dog trotted off to help gather the sheep.

When Gulab came back to the shelter, he saw the tea mug was washed and lying upside down on the low roof. To his utter amazement Kishan was sweeping the doorway of the shelter with a reed jhadu that he had fashioned hurriedly out of the surrounding foliage. His body was bent over double, his head was tilted to a side, the left arm rested on his back, while the right made slow long movements with the broom. It seemed like a ritual dance. Gulab watched him for a while, puzzled and amused by this futile activity that he was engaged in. The inside of the shelter had no constructed floor and was as muddy and grassy as the outside. Kishan pretended not to have seen him and kept sweeping devotedly, tunelessly singing a Bollywood bhajan in accompaniment.

'What are you doing?!' Gulab shouted out at last.

Kishan looked up with sincere eyes. 'Shall I sweep the inside too? I did not want to step in without permission.'

Gulab snatched the broom from him and threw it into the shrubs. 'What do you want?' he asked staring at him directly.

Kishan was not intimidated even though he lowered his eyes, placed his right hand over his mouth and tilted his head in a meditative manner. Unused to such mannered behaviour, Gulab was about to snap at him when he spoke up.

'I want to be your disciple.' Gulab blinked. 'I want to be an anwal like you,' Kishan continued, looking directly at Gulab. 'You are the legendary shepherd of this area. The toughest. The most knowledgeable. One who has fought several storms. One who lives by himself without needing the solace of company.'

Gulab raised a hand to stop him. 'Yes and that's the way I'd like to keep it. Go back the same way you came up.'

But Kishan sat down on his haunches instead, pulling his coat tightly around himself against the cold wind that was blowing uphill.

'Now you will ask why I should be favoured over your son to learn from you, and the answer is this—he is not worthy and has no desire for greatness. I, on the other hand, could be pressing the ripe breasts of girls who throw themselves at me but—' He broke off to look at Gulab, who had let out a laugh.

'How old are you?' Gulab sat down, apparently deciding that he could do with some amusement, and lit a bidi, expertly striking the match, safe from the strong wind, in the cup of his palms.

'How many girls throw themselves at a middle-aged man like you?' he said, spitting out the end of the bidi.

Kishan's gaze froze, as did his train of thought, but recovering quickly, he said, 'I will complete twenty-five years this monsoon.'

Gulab laughed again and looked pointedly at his army clothes.

'I left the army after six months of joining it,' Kishan said. Gulab did not ask why, but he went on to explain, 'My heart was not in it. Firstly, I am a free man, like yourself, and the oppression was unbearable. Secondly, I could not accept the uncouth treatment meted out during the training period. It seems the mother tongue of the army is abuses.'

He let out a volley of insults in imitation of what he had suffered, acting out the poses too, placing his hands on his hips and contorting his face. He cast sidelong glances all through his act but, despite the histrionics, could not coax out a response from Gulab.

He went silent for a moment before getting up and stretching luxuriously. He then moved closer and sat down again, right in front of Gulab. 'I know the work of an anwal is tough, but hardship does not daunt me. I want to live with nature like you do, be my own master and over time earn a flock of sheep. And rest assured, *your* abuses will be acceptable to me,' Kishan said earnestly.

His bidi finished, Gulab got up and went into his shelter.

Kishan sprang up immediately but hesitated and lingered at the doorway.

'I don't want to be paid, just two meals a day will be enough for me.'

It began to drizzle while the sun was still out. 'A jackal is getting married, heh heh, maybe we can partake of the feast too.'

Gulab growled from inside, 'Get going before it becomes a downpour.'

But Kishan did not budge, and soon it was raining hard.

'Don't worry about me; I won't melt,' Kishan said, taking shelter under the narrow roof extension. 'I was born on a night like this. It poured so hard that everyone feared the village would be swept away. Just like the night when Lord Kishan Kanhaiya was born … and so the name. Heh heh … like him I have enough gopis to surround me.' He paused, but failing to elicit a response, he continued, 'It was twenty-five years ago … you could ask your wife,' he added defiantly.

Gulab firmly pulled down a plastic sheet over the doorway to block him and the rain out.

The downpour continued. When evening fell, Gulab peered out and was relieved that Kishan was nowhere in sight. He could contend with nature in all its moods—severe windstorms that swept through these open pastures, the biting cold of snowy winters, and the predators that had to be fended off time and again; such difficulties were routine for him. But he did not have the inclination to engage with humans; the unobtrusive company of his animals was enough for him. The villagers thought of him as irascible and arrogant and whispered rumours about him; he was aware. Women cowered under his unabashed gaze. Whenever he went to the village for supplies, he sensed the squalor of their thoughts, heard the petty ambitions spouting out of their mouths, and found himself hurrying to retreat into the meditative calm of his isolation. When they sought him for wild herbs or sheep wool, he gladly complied as long as there was little interaction. But when they requested to set him up as an exorcist, believing that living in the wild had given him powers over the supernatural, he firmly turned them down. He was a shepherd, not a godman!

It wasn't that he hadn't had encounters of those kind. When he sat near his fire, after having smoked a strong roll, he often heard voices from the past. But that particular vision that he had seen on the pasture on a moonless night several years ago remained a mystery to him. It was perhaps the only time in his life that he had felt deeply frightened. It was a large form, neither human nor animal, that towered over a patch of tall shrubs, devouring one of his sheep. The dogs cowered in silence. He could still hear the squelching of warm flesh and blood, bitten off and chewed slowly in wide jaws. When those dark shiny eyes had turned to look at him, he had retreated hurriedly into his shelter. He emerged the next morning thinking that he had a terrible nightmare only to see dozens of half-eaten carcasses of sheep strewn all over the pasture. It wasn't an animal that would do this, but a demon with an insatiable appetite. Soon after that, there had been massive flooding and landslides in the entire Himalayan region which had caused colossal destruction. The deafening sounds of grating rocks and water had echoed across all the valleys, and those who heard it believed that the end of the world was imminent.

As Gulab lay on his bed of straw and woollen blankets, a continuous bleating kept him from falling asleep. He turned on his solar lamp and got up to inspect. A lamb had a bleeding eye. He washed it with water and decided to go to the higher slopes the next day and gather herbs to treat it. It rained through the night, and the dogs kept growling now and again.

It was still dark when he went outside to relieve himself. When he was getting back to his shelter, the morning sky was clear, and Gulab noticed a form moving towards him from the patch of dense shrubs. It was not the form that had given him sleepless nights a few years ago but a smaller and now familiar figure, shivering and soaked to the bone. Gulab was taken aback by Kishan's audacious tenacity and felt a strange uneasiness return to his stomach. He leapt at him and began to hit him mercilessly with a wet stick that was lying about. A stiff and blue Kishan bent down and accepted the blows on his back, crouching on the ground pathetically, wheezing and coughing. At long last, he turned to look at Gulab with desperate eyes, which in a moment turned accusatory.

While Gulab struggled to light a fire on the wet ground, Kishan gulped down hot tea and hugged a rough woollen blanket to stop the violent shivering. As the fire flared up, he thrust his hands into the flames, finally letting out loud, anguished utterances. When the sun was sufficiently warm, Gulab began to let the sheep out, and Kishan, now somewhat comfortable, attempted to help but was pushed aside and told to run off.

'Yes, yes. I'll be on my way as soon as I have dried off,' he snapped back impertinently and lay down on the grass.

Gulab put out some rice gruel for him to eat in an aluminium bowl, grunting loudly to get his attention, but he needn't have bothered as Kishan was already up and running towards it. He wolfed it down so hungrily that Gulab almost felt sorry for him.

The morning wore on and Kishan spent most of it in a deep slumber out in the sun. Gulab trekked up to the higher slopes after tying the dogs near the sheep, not wanting to risk them attacking Kishan. He hoped that his absence would encourage him to go away and took his time collecting herbs and wild flowers, taking pleasure in their colours and smells.

To his relief, Kishan was nowhere in sight when he returned in the late afternoon. However, he had just finished applying a herbal paste to the lamb's injured eye when Kishan reappeared from the direction of the stream with two pails of water. An annoyed Gulab ignored his ploy to make himself useful and asked him to leave immediately. Kishan merely nodded and went to the back of the shelter. Soon Gulab heard wood being chopped.

By evening, Kishan had chopped a pile of wood logs and cut all the tall grass around the shelter. In these circumstances Gulab felt obliged to invite him in. Gulab watched him warily as he sat near the entrance hugging his knees, staring tragically at the floor. He ate his meal in silence, slurping loudly to indicate his gratitude. When Gulab looked around for a suitable spot for him to sleep, Kishan suggested that he could sleep next to the dogs.

'They will tear you apart,' Gulab growled, not impressed with his attempt to be humble.

'Don't worry, I will be on my way at the crack of dawn,' Kishan muttered, lying down on a woollen blanket near the kitchen fire. 'I don't want to be a burden on anyone.'

He kept sleeping late into the morning. Telling him to go away had become exhausting for Gulab, and he decided to let him stay for a few days. The harsh living conditions would no doubt serve as a deterrent, and he would be gone soon, Gulab assured himself. The pull of a modern lifestyle was too strong for the kind of connection a shepherd must have with nature.

But Kishan hung on, unsurely in the beginning, but settling into his decision every day. Soon he was making morning tea before Gulab was up. He would labour over flavouring the tea carefully with ginger and tulsi, watching Gulab's face eagerly for even a small hint of appreciation. He also offered to roll Gulab's weed but was refused the honour.

Kishan made himself useful in every possible way, and Gulab, who was getting on in years, allowed him to help in the preparations for the impending monsoons. Plenty of wood needed to be gathered, dried and chopped for the stormy cold nights. After the morning chores were done and the sheep had settled into a restful state, Gulab would smoke a roll and spend an hour or two just staring at the valley in silence. Kishan, though quiet, would be restless, his body tense and his face bunched into a frown. When Gulab offered him a drag from his roll, hoping it would ease the nervous energy which continued to make the dogs unfriendly with him, he refused it firmly. In the evening, when Gulab sang in his deep mellifluous voice or played his flute, Kishan, who had no interest in music, would stare into the fire. Gulab wondered what it was he was running away from? What made him so desperate and tenacious? However, he respected each man's right to keep his dark secrets to himself and, thinking of him as a temporary companion, did not give much thought to it.

As the days went by, Kishan, instead of buckling under hardships, became more and more comfortable with his surroundings, and with that, his tongue began to loosen. He would chatter away with the animals, and when Gulab was within earshot, he would slip in some vulgar talk, hankering for a repartee. He often mentioned Gulab's son, comparing himself to him, always showing himself in a favourable light, but sensing Gulab's absolute refusal to engage in that conversation, he had to let go of that thread. Gulab felt irritated with his raspy voice and his insistence on addressing him as 'Bhinjiu', eager to establish a relationship with him.

One particular day as they sat in the pasture, a group of trekkers on their way to the glaciers passed by. Gulab served them refreshments and allowed them to take photographs of him and the sheep. Kishan, however, was hostile and sulky throughout.

After they left he started muttering aggressively, 'These women are polluting our devbhoomi, moving around even when they have their menses. It's because of them that landslides and calamities are recurring. Look at our women; they isolate themselves during that period.'

Gulab asked him where he had heard such drivel.

Surprised to receive a reprimand instead of the approval he had sought, he replied in a low but defiant voice, 'That's what the other shepherds say, Bhinjiu.'

'Then why don't you go and live with them? You've hung around here long enough,' Gulab said, exasperated.

Kishan changed his tone immediately. 'You don't think so? Yes, I guess it's a load of rubbish, women are the earth, from their blood we are born ...' He continued in that vein but Gulab had moved away.

Gulab was aware that other shepherds did speak in this manner. Most of them lived in groups while in the pastures. He was, perhaps, the only shepherd in this area who stubbornly clung on to this ascetic existence. On some days he would have liked to hear the songs—their rustic voices singing in harmonies—but abhorred the other excesses that their evenings were full of.

That day onwards Kishan, as if sensing that his chatter was annoying Gulab and that he was treading on thin ice with him, became as discreet and mute as the grass on the mountainside.

The monsoons were about to set in, and rations for the next three months had to be brought up. Kishan offered to go down to the village for supplies. Gulab was relieved to hand him a list of items and two sheep to sell for money. It did cross his mind that Kishan might run off with the money but decided that it would be a fair price to be rid of him. But Kishan returned, with rations, vulgar gossip and two bottles of alcohol, which he claimed to have bought with his own money. Pulling out the bottles, he began voicing for the first time his objection to ganja. He was shocked when Gulab refused the alcohol and told him that he consumed nothing that didn't grow naturally. Kishan immediately agreed with him but later, sitting outside by himself until dark, proceeded to polish off an entire bottle. Soon, he was shouting into the night about burning the forest down, burning the entire world down, and that they should watch out for him because he never ever forgot a single rebuke. Gulab left him alone in this inebriated state, not wanting to stoke the shouting and ranting. These turned into profuse apologies and explanations the next day which Gulab ignored completely but instructed him to keep alcohol out of his sight henceforth.

The monsoons arrived with a stormy force, wet winds that lashed violently around them and explosive lightening that struck at eye level. Gulab enjoyed watching this extreme drama of nature unfold outside, while he was safe in his shelter with his sheep. But Kishan would cower and swear when the weather became rough.

When Gulab laughed at him, he responded with flattery, 'Not everyone is like you, unafraid, master of everything you see.'

Gulab assured him that he merely knew how to respect nature, but Kishan would have none of it and continued to sing his praises. He spoke of his legendary status in Halbunia village, of how his wife, even though he had abandoned her, continued to wear a mangalsutra and never had a bad word for him. Gulab would fall silent at the mention of his wife but stopped holding it against Kishan for bringing her up. Flattery, even when resisted and recognised for what it is, has a way of enslaving the receiver, and soon on those long days locked in by the rain, the tentacles of Kishan's wily tongue found an anchor in Gulab's heart.

He finally made peace with Kishan's company and was grateful to have someone do anything at his bidding. He took care of the dogs' continued unfriendliness towards Kishan with hard lashes whenever they growled at him. Finally, they submitted to Kishan, who then took over their care too. This newfound leisure made Gulab aware of an old leg injury which had started to bother him, and he was relieved to have his life become physically much easier. Having firmly made his place in Gulab's life, Kishan seemed to breathe easier and went about his chores without coming in Gulab's way.

Gulab began to think of his wife and wondered what she looked like now. More than three decades ago a man from Halbunia village had come to him with his daughter. She had a terrible stomach ache and it didn't take Gulab long to know that she was pregnant. Her father knew too but kept pleading with Gulab to 'make the problem go away'. She had looked at Gulab beseechingly, Sarla, whose youthful beauty had invited an indiscretion from a close relative. When it was discovered, her father had beaten the man out of the village, but she was too far gone into her pregnancy, even though she didn't show much. Not able to offer a solution without endangering her life, Gulab agreed to marry her. He was at a time in his life when the comfort of a household with a beautiful keeper seemed tempting. He was twenty years older than her, but there was enough lust in the marriage to keep him with her for two years or so. A child was born and loved by him as his own. But the demands of a household and her insistence on him giving up his nomadic life, a life he had had since he was a child, had persuaded him to move on. The villager's knew the secret of the child's father but spoke of it in hushed whispers and in their eyes Gulab had done his job in making Sarla a respectable woman. Gulab knew that she did not hold any grudges against him, and he thought of those two years with a fondness. On his way to town for supplies, he would sometimes take a detour to her village to exchange pleasantries, but when his son was old enough to pick fights with him, he began to avoid that route altogether. It had been two decades since he had seen her.

Once autumn set in it was time to move down to lower climes for winter. Gulab was sad at this inevitable parting every year. The fact that few people had seen this part of his world, and that no one knew this immense vista like he did, made him feel a deep kinship with it. It felt like a bond between a parent and a child, or like one between two lifelong friends—unspoken but entwined in each other's consciousness. He would now be moving closer to the village where he owned a patch of land, but here, where he owned nothing, he felt that everything that he could lay his eyes on belonged to him. All winter these slopes would lie hidden under a thick cover of snow, white and dead on the surface but stirring quietly deep under to replenish life and colours for his return in spring.

They began an uneventful trek down to the village. Gulab walked ahead of the pack and was satisfied to see the dogs obediently tailing Kishan at the end of the flock. They first entered the tree cover where strong winds had flattened out the rhododendron trees against the slopes, their trunks smooth and curvy like pale thick snakes tangled on the earth. Further down, the trees became straighter and taller, and the peaks towered higher and higher over the long stretch of the valley, on which the slow parade of the flock seemed like white moving dots. The elegant, green Pindar river had raged in a muddy brown avatar in the monsoons, bursting over, tearing down trees and washing off chunks of slopes, now forcing Gulab and his flock to cut new paths down to the village.

After the rains, work on the road has started again, and it had almost come up to the last house in the village. Gulab felt a twinge as they passed the road workers who were packing up for the day. Late in the evening, they arrived at what was a permanent stone shed, about a kilometre above Barni village. Even though it was at an altitude of 2,500 metres, it felt like they had descended into another world. The air was heavier and the open vista was interrupted by tall deodar and oak trees. Gulab was forced to buy this large piece of land from the village panchayat a few years ago when it sided with the forest department and did not let him graze for free anymore. There was nothing but stacks of wood in the shed, and he left it unlocked on the off chance that someone might want to take shelter for a night. Kishan was very impressed to learn that Gulab owned this piece of land and began measuring it with his footsteps, going all around the boundary twice over.

The din from the road construction made Gulab's thoughts repeatedly return to the open pastures where a timeless rhythm made him forget his own frailty. Here he felt an unsettling sense of foreboding.

Kishan took complete charge of the household and the animals, leaving Gulab plenty of time to ruminate on life and to prepare herbal concoctions to treat villagers who, hearing of his return, came up in droves. Kishan suggested that Gulab charge the villagers, if not in cash, then in kind, but could not convince him. He secretly calculated the money Gulab was forfeiting and the power he could wield if he wished to—like a godman with a cure for every ailment. He daydreamed of becoming Gulab, the rush of adrenaline arousing a deep restlessness within him.

To Kishan's relief, the stream was close to the shed, and fetching water was not a tedious chore anymore. However, the ease he felt here gave him a cocky confidence that set his tongue wagging again. When the village women passed by on their way to the forest, he would suggest that they had eyes for Gulab, not daring to propose himself as the object of their desire. When Gulab laughed it off, Kishan would comment on how virile he was even at his age—strong, lean and handsome—and insist that he could give every one of those Barni men a run for their money.

After finishing the day's work Kishan would wander down to the village and come up in the late evening to cook dinner. Gulab knew he had had alcohol when he was very silent. Otherwise, he had developed a habit of badmouthing the villagers.

And soon he began grumbling about the road. Why should it not come up to their house? They owned the land after all and had every right to demand it. To that, Gulab's reply was that it was good that not every demand be met; if people had their way, they would wish for the river to go past their houses as well. But Kishan argued that the road was already built; what difference would one more kilometre make? Whenever the villagers had a pooja, who did they procure the sacrificial lamb from? Or when they wanted free jadi-booti, wool, meat, or sheep manure, who did they run to? When someone had a snakebite, a vomiting fit or a grievous injury, who came selflessly to their service? Gulab had to simply touch them and they would heal.

'You are God!' he proclaimed as last, as if he had had a sudden revelation.

Gulab let out an uneasy laugh.

Kishan continued. And what did they give Gulab in return? Not a jot of gratitude or a shard of respect. He had worked himself up into quite a temper and continued to rant against the villagers. When Kishan got into these moods Gulab kept quiet, but the man's arguments had begun to leave an impression on him and his dissatisfaction had begun to infect him. But more than that he sensed Kishan's growing restlessness and feared he might leave him. He buried himself into grinding wild turmeric into a fine powder for a child's foot that was festering. His mother had stopped by on her way back from the forest.

Then one day Kishan came back quite drunk and swearing loudly, a deep cut on his hand and a bruise on his forehead. Gulab immediately tended to his wounds.

'They have gone too far this time, Bhinjiu! You know what that gram pradhan's boy said today? Thinks no end of himself that motherfucker. He said that rather than copulating with your wife you had chosen to copulate with sheep.'

Gulab was stung by that remark.

'I will not stand by silent anymore and hear this humiliating talk about a selfless man like yourself.'

And he began to sob. Gulab gently chided Kishan and urged him not to go down to the village. Kishan replied that there was no pleasure in drinking alone. After a moment of calculated silence, he pulled out a quarter bottle from his pocket, poured a small drink into a glass and slid it towards Gulab.

'If you agree to have just one small drink with me every evening, I promise not to go down to the village except to buy supplies.'

When Gulab refused, Kishan sulked and watched him with hurt eyes. Finally, Gulab sighed and picked up the drink and sipped at it slowly. Kishan settled down next to him with deep satisfaction and drank straight from the bottle.

While Kishan muttered in his sleep, Gulab lay awake that night. He had always been at odds with the villagers, mainly over grazing rights and also because of his objection to the road being made in this landslide prone area. But that had not come in the way of him tending to their maladies whatever time of night or day. Kishan was right; they ought to have at least asked him about the road, as they ought to have had enough decency to not engage in loose talk about him.

Kishan kept his word. He stopped going down to the village. Instead, he settled down near the kitchen fire every evening with Gulab, progressively pouring him stiffer drinks till Gulab began looking forward to the daily dose, glad to have Kishan in sight all the time. Kishan alternated between muttering obscenities about the villagers and lapsing into long spells of glumness.

And in this company Gulab felt his own despondence grow steadily. Thoughts of mortality and an acute awareness of his advancing years made him anxious, keeping him up some nights, fearful of not waking up the next morning.

Kishan looked after him diligently, but his manner towards Gulab had changed—flattery had given way to an authoritative air. And again, he started making the demand for the road to come up to their shed and would not let go of it. An enfeebled Gulab began to feel nervous—all he wanted was for Kishan to stay. When he didn't respond at all to Kishan's ranting, the latter stomped out of the shed.

'Are you afraid of these villagers?' he thundered. 'That cretin son of the gram pradhan … I could strangle him with one hand.' He came back into the kitchen.

His blood-red eyes caught light from the fire, and his raspy voice hissed across the darkness. 'I have no fear of anyone, let me tell you. I am already up for fifteen years in prison if they ever find me.' Gulab was not completely surprised to hear this.

Kishan continued, 'Arson and manslaughter were the words they kept repeating as they carried on the investigation. Truth is, I could not take the goddamn army trainer's abuses any longer.' Now he came and squatted across the fire from Gulab, staring at him threateningly.

'That day, the trainer was sick and sleeping in his room. I entered the barracks in the middle of the afternoon when the marathon training was on ...' He paused to chuckle. 'Ashes ... that's what was left of the entire building and the fifteen men inside it. I still fantasise about the trainer's screams as his body burnt to a crisp.' His breath scraped the brief silence. 'They could not find any evidence, and I left for home, saying my father was ill. But that bastard father of mine greeted me with scorn, smelt something fishy, and kept threatening to call the police. I had to leave my own house, but not before I broke his legs with a cricket bat.' Now he flashed his perfect set of teeth at Gulab. 'I had always wanted to come and live with you since I was a little boy ... I am so glad that dream has come true. But I will not rest till that road comes up to our house. I'm going to block the stream down to the village till that happens.'

Gulab fixed his gaze on the crackling embers, refusing to look at the crazy eyes that were challenging him.

The next day when Kishan rolled a large log of wood into the stream to block its flow down to the village, Gulab kept silent. In the next few days, the villagers came and removed the log to release the water, but Kishan just blocked it off again. Gulab tried to reason with him. The area was landslide-prone, a road would weaken the hillside and precipitate a disaster. But Kishan refused to back down.

While the process of entanglement can be slow sometimes, the moment of disenchantment is often sudden. And as Gulab looked at Kishan bent over the fire that night, humming a bhajan tunelessly as was his wont, he felt a violent revulsion at the sight of this reprehensible being. He cringed at his own folly, the fatal flaw of pride, of accepting obeisance from the devil that he had given in to. But it was not too late.

He drew himself up to his full height, looked directly at the pathetic creature before him and declared, 'The road will not come up to the shed under my watch. That is my final word.'

But it *was* too late. He was so drunk that he collapsed back to the ground.

A shocked Kishan watched him guardedly, not reacting for some time. *The time has come!* He got up and looked down at the feeble old shepherd, his eyes glittering with insanity. With the ferocity of a cornered animal, he picked up a pair of tongs that were heating in the fire, rushed towards Gulab and plunged them into his eyes.

'There!' he declared, 'Now, it won't happen under your watch!'

Gulab's anguished screams were drowned by the loud desperate pleas of the madman who was now begging for forgiveness. He crouched next to Gulab and promised fervently to take care of him forever. His hands hovered uncertainly over the ruined face before settling on Gulab's shoulders.

'You will never have to see again,' he whispered hoarsely, as if offering comfort. 'I will be your eyes forever.'

The fire crackled behind them, throwing their shadows large and distorted against the rock wall, until it was impossible to tell which was the man and which the monster.

Barni was no longer a forgotten village; it had transformed into a prosperous township. Cement houses, which doubled up as hotels, had sprouted haphazardly all over the hillside. Crowds thronged here from all over the country. The tarred road which often experienced terrible traffic snarls went right up to what used to be a shepherd's shed.

Except it was not a shed anymore. It was an ashram. The godman would be seated in a special room constructed for him, his forehead smeared with ash and his body swathed in a large orange robe. Around him milled several helpers keeping the seekers in order.

In a small cell in the basement of the triple-storey structure, Gulab, his foot chained to an iron peg, would sit on the floor, a permanent darkness all around him. In his highly inebriated state, he would smell the herbs and grind them to medicinal concoctions, to the best of his ability. But it was not his medicines that healed the throng of humanity who stood outside the shed carrying offerings in their arms; it was the deep faith they carried in their hearts.

The villagers had initially resisted paying obeisance to the self-declared godman who they knew to be the drunkard Kishan. They had heard rumours about his dubious past, and many had had unpleasant interactions with him. However, it was impossible to have access to Gulab's herbal medicines without going past him and making an offering. They were surprised to see how quickly word spread and people began coming in flocks, seeking relief from their maladies. And when the villagers smelt money, which the droves of believers were bringing in, they were more than willing to establish a new truth. After meditating for several years in the upper Himalayas, the godman had received enlightenment, they said. Wishing to serve humanity, he had deigned to descend to Barni village.

Gulab is in a pasture tending to a lamb. It is neither day nor night. He hears the squelching of flesh and blood. He turns to see a hideous being amidst the brush, devouring a human body. The demon raises its head to look at Gulab, still chewing with its wide bloodied jaws. Gulab finds that he is looking at himself. Startled, he drops the lamb, and it rolls off the edge of the cliff.

He woke up in a sweat, his mouth wet and salty, the darkness of the cell weighing down on him. For the first time in years, he did not reach for the bottle. He sat very still, listening.

The sky thundered over the valley, and the earth rumbled in response. The rain began to pour down with a vengeance and continued for seven days and seven nights. The hillside, cut, scarred and hollowed out over years, heaved, then gave way. The landslide rushed down and buried the entire slope. Everyone in the village was taken in their sleep. The ashram, the road, the cement houses, the offerings, the secrets the villagers had guarded so carefully, were folded back into mud and stone. There were no cries for help, no one to give an account of how the mountain had moved.

When the rescue team finally arrived, there were no signs of life. As they climbed through the rubble, they heard the 'baas' of sheep ringing through the forest, drifting from somewhere higher up the slope.

That night, by the campfire, a group of rescuers reported seeing a tall lone figure standing on a ridge, looking down at the ruined valley below.

By morning there was no trace of him.

The Monkey Chaser

They stood outside the fencing that marked the boundary of the apple orchard. Ganesh tapped idly on the board which read 'Viceroy Estate' and, assuming a mild frown, muttered to himself, moving his finger around in the air as if he was making some important calculations and contemplating on outcomes. He stole a glance at Prema and, nervous that she was slipping away, grabbed her hand. She stiffened and tried to withdraw, but he refused to let go.

'Do you know that this entire hillside, right up to that peak, belonged to us,' he said. 'And since that is a forest,' he said, pointing to the hillside across the valley, 'you could say that everything you can set your eyes on right now was ours.'

'Look, look …' he repeated, insisting that Prema follow his finger, which pointed to the entire expanse around him. Anticipating her disbelief, he let out an elated chuckle. 'I bet you haven't seen so many trees in your life. I hear in Rudrapur you only have tall buildings.'

Prema managed to withdraw her hand from his sweaty clasp and wiped it on her kurta.

Unfazed he continued, 'We grew wheat and rice on these terraced fields. Harvest was a back-breaking time for all of us. But now these outsiders have planted only fruit trees. Maybe they will open a resort soon and I can become the manager.'

Prema looked longingly at the path that they had come up from, wanting to turn back.

Noting her mood, Ganesh added quickly, 'Mummy said you are a very nice girl, that we would be a perfect match for each other.'

'Is that what you call your mother, not Ija like everyone else does around here?' Prema replied with a mocking smile.

'What do you call your mother?' He asked, not sure what to make of her tone.

After an awkward silence he pointed to the orchard. 'These people from Delhi, Punjabi Aroras, bought the whole hillside from my father for five lakh rupees. Today it's worth crores—I couldn't buy it back if I wanted to.' He said this not with regret but pride, as if past ownership of this precious piece of land made him a worthy match.

'Why did you sell it all and keep such a small portion for yourself?' Prema asked.

'Oh, that was for Hema di's wedding. My great grandfather, who was a sarpanch in his time, visited Papa's dream and instructed him to arrange a grand wedding.'

His tone had become imperious. 'Papa often had prophetic dreams.' After a pause he added, 'I have inherited that from him; I too can sense signs, read signals ...'

Not sure how to interpret the strange manner in which Prema was looking at him, he proceeded to add a logical explanation: 'With Hema di gone it would have been impossible for Mummy to cultivate the fields on her own anyway.'

'Could you not have helped her?' she asked with rising disaffection.

He ignored the question. 'It was a grand wedding. Eight hundred people feasted on mutton of sheep that had fed on soft, tender grass high up in the bugyals. The shepherd vouched for that. The DJ ensured that the entire valley was filled with music for three whole days, and an entire acre around the house was decorated with lights. Not a single baraati was in his senses on the wedding day! The groom drank so much he tumbled off the horse!' He clapped his hands with glee.

She looked baffled. 'All the money was spent on the wedding?'

He took a moment to respond to what sounded like an accusation. 'Of course there was some money left over, with which Papa bought himself a bike.'

'And where is that bike now?' Prema asked with a glimmer of hope.

'Oh, that went with him.' He had perked up again. 'He would not move without his bike, not a single step, and you could see him zipping around the hillside all day, even when he had had a few ...' here he made a gesture to indicate a drink. 'He flew off the edge of the mountain on it. The bike, as well as his body was completely mangled.'

Noting her alarm, he proceeded to explain, 'Papa did not die of a snake bite, or an organ dysfunction like most people do. He literally flew off into the sunset on his bike, like a king on his throne.'

Prema shook her head and began to move down the slope. Ganesh dashed after her.

'Are you upset? Ours will be a grand wedding too.'

'I will accept this proposal only when you get yourself a regular job.' Her voice was clipped.

He dropped his jaw in a comical manner and moved his pupils from side to side. 'Did you hear that?' he whispered. 'It's a tiger close by.'

Prema looked at him incredulously, her eyes wide with impatience.

'It's so easy to scare you city people!' he cackled nervously. 'Darling, listen—'

Prema snapped at him, 'I am not your darling! We have only just met.' She continued in a calmer voice, 'If you still had the land, we could have cultivated it together, sold the produce, had enough to ...'

He cut her short. 'Where is the water to cultivate the land? And who works so hard these days? I'll ask to be the manager of the resort these orchard people are going to open. It will be clean work—shout at people, make phone calls, greet guests, coat-tie ...'

As he acted out his reverie, Prema laughed out loud. His small, thin figure engaged in such grandstanding cut such a sorry picture.

'Call me when you land that job.' She turned and, before he could stop her again, ran down the path.

Ganesh did not even attempt to follow her this time. Instead, he collapsed onto a grassy patch, watching her move towards his house which was further down the slope. 'As if you are some goddess,' he muttered petulantly. 'Your father is merely a security guard in a factory.'

A snake slithered by in the grass. Is that a good omen or a bad one, he wondered to himself as he beat the grass with a stick. Soon he saw that his mother had come out to see Prema and her father off.

'Look back, Prema. Look back if you love me,' he whispered in the fashion of many films he had seen. He watched her hopefully till she disappeared down the slope.

He sat staring at the valley till it was almost dark. When he got home, Mummy, as he chose to call her, was watching a TV serial while shelling peas. Ganesh began popping shelled peas into his mouth while asking her to fill him in on plot details. When she did not reply at all, he became sulky.

'So, when will you fix the wedding date, Mummy?' he asked, tugging at her sleeve.

'It doesn't look promising to me,' she replied without taking her eyes off the television screen. Then in a sterner tone she added, 'Now don't you start chasing this Prema girl; we'll find someone else for you.'

He continued to sulk. *Nothing seemed to work out, did it?* Last year he had set up a chai shop on the highway with a fantastic view of the river. However, because it was on a sharp bend, cars rarely stopped there. Very soon it became a gambling spot for locals, who ran up bills but never paid. He had to shut shop after just three months. Most of the stock was still stored in the house. Mummy was getting fat going through packets of chips and cheese balls. Then came the orchard idea. Inspired by the orchard above, he planted saplings of an exotic apple variety. No one told him they needed protection from the snow, and they died that winter. The biggest blow came when he heard that Aarti, the local sweetheart, was engaged. He declared a hadtaal for a week, refusing to eat, bathe or shave, hoping word of his devotion would reach her. However, when he had a fainting spell, Mummy force-fed him. He was angry with her for having ruined his well-laid plan of gaining sympathy. Later he made a fine show of enjoying Aarti's wedding. However, rejection by Prema, such an ordinary looker, felt altogether unacceptable.

'I will get a job soon, Mummy, and Prema will be your bahu.' Mummy nodded, hiding the despair she felt for him.

He woke up cheerful the next morning. Sparrows twittered outside his window, and a scarlet rose had bloomed on the bush that adorned their otherwise unassuming home. He wore his brightest jacket and took his time styling his hair. Mummy watched him in suspicious silence before warning him against trouble.

Untouched by her misgivings, Ganesh walked out briskly and began to climb up the slope, whistling, past the orchard and towards the grand house atop the hill. As a child he had spent hours on this hilltop, which until a few years ago had been nothing but wilderness.

The dog inside began to bark as he approached the door. The gardener hurried towards him and, with a familiar gesture, nodded upwards and twirled his open hand like a flower, demanding to know what on earth Ganesh wanted.

'I'm here to meet Aunty,' Ganesh replied haughtily.

'Aunty who?'

'Mrs Arora, who bought this land from us.' *That should put him in his place*, he thought.

Instead, Madhav Ram looked at him with open scorn. 'You mean *Madam*? What do you want with her?'

Ganesh did not deign to reply. With his hands clasped behind his back, he began inspecting the house with a sense of proprietorship. From the corner of his eye, he saw Madhav Ram watch him for a moment before disappearing inside.

Noticing that the door was ajar, Ganesh stepped in unannounced. He was instantly flattened by a bouncy golden dog that launched itself on him and began licking his face. After a fuss, the dog was restrained. Mrs Arora explained apologetically that the dog's attack had been one of friendly enthusiasm. Relieved to hear that Ganesh shook off the episode with a shrill, nervous laugh.

He extended his hand, which she accepted with surprise. It was then that she recognised him, having seen him hanging around the hillside on her way to the market. Ganesh plonked himself into a sofa chair opposite her. Madhav Ram gasped and began to protest, but Mrs Arora silenced him with a look. She turned to Ganesh expectantly, but he returned Madhav Ram's gaze with a cold stare, making it clear that he would not speak in his presence. Reading the moment, Mrs Arora nodded to the gardener to leave with the dog.

Ganesh observed her closely. He was surprised to see her dressed so plainly. Her hair was unkempt, and her slippers were old and frayed. The sight emboldened him.

'Aunty, I'm here for the manager's job at the resort you are opening,' he blurted out. 'I don't have experience but I'm a graduate. And we can negotiate the salary. After all, we're practically family.'

She looked at him blankly. 'But we are not opening a resort. Where did you hear that?'

'Everyone seems to be opening one around here. It's good business,' Ganesh said.

'I'm quite happy with the orchard and my peace,' Mrs Arora replied.

Disconcerted by her polite firmness and suddenly awkward to be seated across from her, Ganesh began to massage his knees.

Mrs Arora's phone rang in the next room. She called out to her help, but when there was no response, she stepped away to take the call.

Left alone, Ganesh wandered about the room, feigning interest in the books on the shelves and the painting on the wall. He studied it from different angles, unable to make sense of it. Perhaps it was hung upside down, he thought, craning his head to inspect it, which is exactly how Mrs Arora found him when she returned. He began to point out the oversight to her, but she cut him short, curtly saying she had something urgent to attend to and suggesting that he leave.

He muttered an apology, half extended his hand to shake hers, then awkwardly folded it into a namaste before hurrying out.

On the way back, the snowy peaks that had refreshed him in the morning were now veiled by dark clouds. A familiar dissatisfaction settled into Ganesh.

He stole some money from Mummy and went down to the marketplace. Instead of drinking, as he had planned, he gambled away the petty change.

The next morning, as Mrs Arora paid her staff, she realised that two thousand rupees were missing. She was certain of the amount she had withdrawn only days earlier. After searching her handbag and the house, she carefully retraced her actions the previous day. Her staff had no access to her wardrobe, and the only time her bag had been left unattended on the mantlepiece above the fireplace was when Ganesh had barged in. By evening, her doubt had hardened into resolve. If she was to feel safe in this wilderness, she would have to confront neighbours with a taste for petty theft. She decided to go to his house.

Ganesh had no immediate response to the accusation. As Mrs Arora stood there with Madhav Ram, refusing to leave without an explanation, he began to speak of an ancestor who once guarded gold for the local raja, back when there were no banks, and from whose keeping not a single coin had ever gone missing.

Mummy, who had been washing vessels, overheard the exchange and came across, wiping her hands, ready to take on these outsiders.

'Listen, Arora Memsaheb,' she said, 'I can vouch for my son's unbending honesty. He does not have the imagination for crookery. I can swear on Golu Devta! You may fault him for presumptuousness and far-fetched daydreaming, I will concede that much, but not for dishonesty.'

'I want to make it clear that I will not have any kind of hanky-panky around my property; otherwise there will be consequences.' Mrs Arora wanted to sound firm, but her voice wavered. She began to move away, embarrassed to have been drawn into the matter at all.

Madhav Ram, however, continued to berate Ganesh, urging him to return the money at once so that no one else's honesty would be brought into question. An argument broke out between him and Mummy, but Ganesh slipped away, disappearing into the forest.

Mummy was stung by the accusations. That night when Ganesh came home, she urged him to find some regular work so people would stop speaking ill of him.

'Look at your cousins,' she said. 'One is a police officer, another a big businessman. And here you are, being accused of petty theft by people who bought their land from us.'

Ganesh wanted to point out that the parents of those cousins had prospered early and sent their children to English-medium schools, but he said nothing. The unease in his stomach deepened, and soon he found himself drinking every day to take care of it.

A few weeks later, while emptying her handbag, Mrs Arora discovered the missing note she had accused Ganesh of stealing, tucked away in a recess. She was seized by guilt, and despite Madhav Ram's advice to let the matter rest, she felt compelled to set it right at once. She sent word for Ganesh to come over.

Though surprised and gracious at first in accepting her apology, Ganesh soon grew self-righteous and repeated the story of his ancestor who had once guarded a raja's gold. If not even a single coin had gone missing then, why would he, Ganesh, that ancestor's descendant, stoop to pilfering mere rupees?

Mrs Arora listened patiently as he sat across from her, slurping his tea. At his insistence it was made with undiluted milk and heavy sugar. It was his one indulgence, he informed her; otherwise, his mother struggled to make him eat even two rotis.

Mrs Arora, still stung by remorse, began, 'About the job ...'

'Are you opening a resort?' She shook her head, uncertain. 'Everything else is taken care of, but there is one thing you could handle. Monkeys have become a real menace in the orchard. If you could chase them away... I mean, if you could oversee the orchard, I would be very grateful.' She waited, awkwardly, for his response.

Ganesh said nothing. He stared intently at her left shoulder for a long moment, making her uneasy. Chasing monkeys? No coat and tie, no people to order about. But *Overseer of the Viceroy Estate* sounded impressive enough to tell Prema.

He looked up abruptly. 'Salary?'

She hesitated. 'Five thousand rupees a month?'

He rolled the figure around in his head. It was not much, but it was something.

'And, of course,' she said, almost as an afterthought, 'you will have Bosco to help you.'

Hearing his name, the golden retriever trotted over with a bone in his mouth. Today he did not bother to bark at Ganesh. Mrs Arora patted him and spoke indulgently, as one would to a beloved child.

'We only want to chew on our bone all day, don't we? And do ninni in the sun.' Seeing the dog so favoured, the idea of having him as a companion suddenly appealed to Ganesh. He got up abruptly.

'So, nine o'clock tomorrow morning?'

'Oh no,' she said. 'Much earlier. The monkeys start their business at the crack of dawn, as you know. Six o'clock would be best. You can rest in the afternoon, and then work three hours again in the evening.'

It sounded excessive to Ganesh, but he decided to accept the job in good faith. A good relationship with the lady would ensure that he would be made manager when the resort came up, as he was sure it would one day.

On his way down, he called Prema repeatedly until she picked up. He informed her of his new position—Manager of Viceroy Estate—and added that the salary was still being negotiated. He would be in charge of the orchards and of the sales and marketing of the fruit.

He liked the word 'marketing'. It had an important ring to it. A distant cousin worked in marketing for a medicine company in Delhi.

He threw in some sweet talk. Prema said she had exams and hung up.

Mummy was pleased that Mrs Arora had seen the folly of her ways and felt hopeful for her son.

Ganesh soon found that the job was not as cushy as it sounded, though he took to it with gusto. The orchard was vast, and its fruit invited a steady stream of unwanted guests.

There were hordes of rhesus monkeys, brown-furred with red faces, captured from the Tarai plains at the behest of influential farmers and released into the mountain forests. And then there were the indigenous langurs, white-furred with black faces, more menacing but less destructive than the former.

The monkeys, used to the dog and fond of teasing him from the treetops, were startled by the sight of a human hurtling down the slope towards them, swinging a stick and howling at the top of his voice. Bosco followed at a distance, trotting obligingly, stopping now and then to sniff the grass. The monkeys retreated into the neighbouring jungle for a few hours before returning again.

With the orchard briefly cleared, Ganesh turned his wrath on the birds, clapping his hands furiously till they were red and stinging, while Bosco lay down in the sun and gnawed at his bone. Ganesh had never felt so useful in his life, not even at his sister's wedding, where he had been assigned the task of grating gur for the halwa. He had applied himself so earnestly that he grated the tops of his fingers and had to abandon the job.

He became quite fond of the dog who greeted him with great enthusiasm every morning. They would run up and down the hillside, with Bosco taking the lead, before resting under a tree.

In the orchard, Bosco was entirely at Ganesh's command. He wasn't a dog, he told Mummy at dinner, he was a lion, with a shiny golden coat and a fulsome mane! And at home he didn't simply curl up anywhere; he had a special bed with a soft satin mattress. His lunch came from a fancy packet: hard kibbles doused in a fresh curry with large chunks of meat.

'Heck! If I had been in the least interested in food, I might have wished to exchange places with Bosco.' He chuckled while Mummy grimaced and urged him to have another hot roti.

Mrs Arora's staff was displeased with this arrangement. Madhav Ram prickled at having to give up partial control of Bosco and, having taken great care to learn the correct pronunciation of his name, resented that Ganesh insisted on calling him Shera, a common name for dogs in the hills. What was more infuriating was that the dog responded to that name with enthusiasm.

The cleaner, a local from the village, bristled at Ganesh's attempts at familiarity because of the accidental circumstance of being the original landowner. He addressed Mrs Arora as 'aunty' and shouted western greetings to her on his way in and out. Mrs Arora, however, took no offence. She was pleased that the monkeys were being driven away. This year she would have a good harvest of apples.

The restlessness that often racked Ganesh had been temporarily stilled by physical exertion and the sheen of a new job. After a few weeks, however, it began to creep back. The resting periods between his excursions became longer and longer. Often, he merely threw a stick for the dog to fetch, driving off a few monkeys in the bargain. The monkeys, once startled by his charge, now leapt from tree to tree, teasing him as they had teased the dog. More than anything else, used as he was to being the master of his own time, he began to resent having to rise so early each morning.

Prema never called back. His messages went unanswered too.

Madhav Ram, who kept a keen eye on him, reported him to Mrs Arora after he found him taking long naps during work hours. She ignored it at first, but nagged by regular complaints from the staff, she was forced to speak to him.

Though Ganesh was accustomed to being reprimanded, he would have liked her tone to have been less authoritative. He held his tongue, not wanting to gratify Madhav Ram, and laughed it off, saying he had been unwell and there would be no cause for complaint again.

However, he could not shake off the ennui that had set in, even as he attempted to renew his enthusiasm. He was listless with Bosco too, no longer responding to his greetings, shoving him aside when he whined for attention. Mrs Arora's sharp words and the sniggers of her staff replayed in his head like a looped reel, each pass heightening his humiliation.

It was a hot autumn afternoon. Bosco had wandered off. After a brief, vicious chase through the orchard, Ganesh had stretched out under a tree and drifted into sleep. He felt a tap on his shoulder. Irritated, he rolled onto his stomach, unwilling to surface from the nap. The tap came again. He half-opened his eyes. A large langur sat beside him, its black face inches from his own, its white, shaggy body almost brushing him. Ganesh froze. They stared at each other for several long seconds. The langur did not blink.

If this fellow bites me, Ganesh thought, *the old lady will have to pay for the injections ... She'll also have to give me compensation ... enough to buy a bike, perhaps. Prema will be impressed.*

The langur twitched its face ever so slightly and bared a narrow flash of white teeth. Ganesh's heart pounded. He was about to bolt when the ape gripped his shoulder, sprang into a tree in a single fluid movement and vanished. Ganesh lay where he had fallen, his limbs prickling, his skin alive. As his heartbeat slowed, a troubling certainty settled into him—something had passed between them. *What had the creature recognised in him?*

He turned onto his back and lay staring at the canopy above and contemplated the encounter. What a magnificent creature it was, and how absurd he must look, flailing at it with a stick every morning and evening. The thought left a faint heat in his chest, something close to shame. Slowly, another certainty took shape. The langur, like him, belonged to these hills. Unlike the red-faced monkeys dragged up from the plains, it had a rightful claim to the orchard, to the fruit, and to the land itself. To drive it away was an error. It was the outsiders who had no business being here.

His thoughts slid, almost naturally, to Mrs Arora, to the way she had ticked him off before her staff. This land had fed his forefathers for generations, and now she had arrived with her money and her rules, certain she could order anyone as she pleased. That could not be allowed.

He picked up his stick and began walking towards the main house. He had no definite plan. Only a vague idea that the rising sting of the dissatisfaction, which was increasingly eating into him, must be put to rest. Bosco trotted alongside him, barking for attention.

Mrs Arora was pruning her geraniums in the garden. She smiled when she saw him approaching, looked at him for a moment, then bent down to pet Bosco. Ganesh stood behind her, taking in the white crown of her head bent before him, the soft, wrinkled neck, the skin so thin that a web of blue veins showed through it. If he brought the stick down, the head would split open, he thought, like a watermelon.

She straightened suddenly. His breath was shallow. The stick felt heavy in his hand.

He lowered it.

'I'm thirsty,' he stuttered. 'Bring me some water.' She began to call out to the cook, but he cut her short.

'No, you get me the water … ' he faltered, then added hopelessly, 'I … I … want you to bring it.'

She looked at him sharply. Madhav Ram, who had come up behind her, was making aggressive gestures, muttering, asking Ganesh if he had got possessed by a demon or won a lottery. Ganesh stared past them, whistling tunelessly, his grip tightening around the stick.

Mrs Arora said nothing. She dropped her gardening gloves and went inside. Left standing there, Ganesh became fidgety and without any thought brought the stick down on a patch of irises, striking them again and again. Madhav Ram cried out and leapt at Ganesh. He seized the other end of the stick and tried to wrench it away from him. Ganesh held on with all his might. The staff rushed in, voices rising, hands grabbing. The struggle ended only when the stick snapped in two and both men staggered back, Madhav Ram falling heavily to the ground.

Mrs Arora returned with a glass of water on a tray and handed it to Ganesh. He drank it in one go and set the glass back with a deliberate thump. She met his gaze, then handed him an envelope.

'Count it later,' she said. 'It's your full month's pay.'

There was a pause.

'This settles everything,' she added.

Ganesh turned and began walking down the hill. He could feel their eyes on his back. He heard Madhav Ram calling out, restraining Bosco.

His stride lengthened, each step striking the ground hard. He told himself that he did not care about Prema. She was ordinary. Very ordinary. Marriage itself was a trap, and he had managed well enough on his own. Mummy's face rose before him, already anxious, already disappointed. What right had she ever had to decide anything for him? If she had fed him better, and pushed him harder, he would not have grown up to be scrawny and short, so easy to dismiss.

By the time he reached the orchard gate, his anger had tightened into resolve—he would bring every villager who owed him money to task. If they did not comply, he would damage their property. He wrenched the board that read 'Viceroy Estate' from its posts and stamped on it until it splintered.

Bosco had managed to break free and ran after him. However, when he saw him stomping on the board, he was confused and began barking loudly. Ganesh turned and kicked him hard. The dog yelped, then growled. Ganesh quickened his steps, leaving the scene behind.

As he neared his house, his anger had thinned out, leaving behind a dull, empty calm. The thought of sleeping late the next morning pleased him. He stopped beneath the oak tree above his house and looked out at the valley. The afternoon sun had flooded it with yellow light. A breeze passed over the hillside, stirring a soft, restless whisper through the grass. Ganesh leaned back against the trunk. From his house below, a melodramatic musical track could be heard. Mummy was watching the afternoon soap. When he closed his eyes, sleep came quickly.

Amma's Keys

Laxman's eyes wandered back to the path again as he stirred tea leaves into the large black kettle. The motorable road ended in Khadkiya, a few kilometres away. From there the walking path unravelled across the hillside, passing Laxman's dhaba cum general store. The light was fading fast, but there was still no sign of Amma, his grandmother. The baraatis were filtering back in twos and fours, bursting with details of the grand wedding. Village weddings never allowed for such elaborate arrangements, and Gopal da, the groom's father, had done well to insist that it be held in the nearest town. While the menfolk had attended in full strength, most women, including Laxman's wife, were busy with the harvest. Laxman also had to stay back in the village as he was to receive supplies for his shop that very day. Amma, however, who never let a chance for revelry slip by, had set off early that morning, forgetting the painful knee she had complained of the night before.

When Laxman's wife, Rekha, had tried to warn her of the long walk, Amma had replied sharply, 'Are my legs broken that I should stay back? Gopal came twice to invite me, and someone from the family ought to attend.'

When it seemed that the last baraati had staggered back, Laxman began to make casual inquiries about Amma, not wanting to display his anxiety yet. As it is, she had caused him enough embarrassment. Her exuberance, while spoken of with indulgence by the villagers, was a source of mirth for everyone in the village, and Laxman was quick to detect that hint of sarcasm when Amma's 'lovable' exploits were discussed freely in his dhaba.

The men were so drunk that no one could give a clear answer about her whereabouts, but someone declared with confidence that Harish had not returned. He had stopped to buy rations at Bharadi, and Amma would certainly be with him. That should have relieved Laxman, but instead he felt a sharp prick of irritation. Did he not stock enough rations that Harish should have to lug them all the way from Bharadi just to save a few rupees? When that feeling passed, he began to watch the path again, which was now a ribbon of moonlight. At long last Harish's ghostly form appeared in the distance, Amma in tow. Laxman breathed easy and began to frame in his head the scoldings he would shower on her. The mild worry Amma had caused became an excuse for the men to linger on and order several rounds of tea, and Laxman began to diligently keep track of the money owed to him.

However, when Harish came closer, it became apparent that it was not Amma at all, but a sack of supplies he was lugging on his back. There was an uproar which confused Harish, and he dumped the sack inside the shop. Even in his consternation Laxman peered into it. A can of oil and a bag of flour, at a quick glance. Returning to the urgent matter at hand, Laxman turned to Harish and with unexpected harshness began bombarding him with questions about Amma, as if Harish was responsible for her whereabouts. Harish's intoxication evaporated immediately as he defended himself and declared that he had not seen Amma at all that day.

When it was clear that everyone was back in the village, the men began to recount Amma's movements through the day. Chamu had last seen her when she had taken centre stage at the wedding, dancing at length to a string of pahadi songs. Everyone chimed in that they had clapped along and agreed that her presence had added much colour to the baraat. As an aside Chamu told Laxman that Kamlesh Bubu had tried to upstage Amma by doing exaggerated Bollywood moves. Everyone agreed that those pelvic thrusts would have suited his teenage grandson better. Rajesh reported that he had served Amma seconds and thirds at the reception that followed and had later seen her at the sweets counter piling up her plate. Everyone agreed that even though the food was not up to the mark, the desserts had been exceptional. There was no record of Amma after the feast.

As the murmur about Amma being missing gained momentum, more people gathered in the shop, and the tea kettle was not rested for a moment. At this point, an anxious Laxman, while trying to piece together Amma's movements through the day, raised his voice and told everyone sharply to pay for their teas. This caused half the crowd to disperse. Those who stayed back were trying to make phone calls to the groom and his family, who were coming back to the village the next day, feeling certain that they would have persuaded Amma to stay back with them, the dear heart that she was. Even though the signal was weak and the calls were not going through, Laxman was beginning to relax in the belief that Amma had probably just stayed back when Kanta came in to buy sugar. She was one of the few women who had gone for the wedding. Being sober and completely in her senses, she was able to clearly state that she saw Amma taking a pillion ride on a stranger's scooter. Who that person was or how far he would have given Amma a ride, Kanta was unable to say. She added, with a smirk, that she had requested Amma to accompany her and the small group of women at the wedding in taking a jeep ride to Khadkiya, but Amma had paid no heed.

'Why should I stay with you dullards when I can fly away like a bird with this young man,' Amma had said as she zipped off with the stranger, clinging onto him, her ghaghra flying freely in the wind.

There were some muted sniggers. A peeved Laxman lashed out at everyone, saying that he should never have allowed Amma to go without him, trusting all of them as he did. There was a guilty hush before Laxman spun into action. He doused the fire in the choolah, noted down the cups of tea that were not paid for, locked the shop hurriedly and, accompanied by a large group, set off for Khadkiya.

Everyone had sobered down—the thought of Amma in trouble had taken care of that—and they walked cautiously down the long distance of the narrow path, thankful for the moonlit night. Various theories were being knocked around. Had the stranger robbed Amma of her gold jewellery and abandoned her midway? ... Or done something worse? Such crimes were not uncommon now, even in the hills. Several people from the plains had moved into the area and infested it with crime … otherwise pahadis were such simple honest folk. *Or* had she charmed the scooter rider so utterly that he had insisted on her taking a break in his house for the night? Who could that person be? No one they knew owned a scooter in the neighbouring villages.

Reaching Khadkiya, they woke up everyone in the marketplace, but no one had any news of Amma. A drunk jeep driver was shaken out of his sleep with difficulty, but hearing that Amma was missing, he jumped into action. After a brief tussle, a search party of eight people was finalised—those in their best senses—and soon the jeep took off in the direction of the town where the wedding had taken place.

After about twenty minutes of driving, waking two households along the road for inquires and disturbing the forest birds with calls for Amma, Mohan suddenly remembered that a man in Karmi village, about fifteen kilometres away, owned a scooter. That was a flash of hope, because the man was local and would never harm Amma. The driver stepped on the pedal making the jeep jump dangerously up in the air. Laxman's anxiety eased for a moment, only to be replaced by irritation. Could Kanta not have been more persuasive and got Amma along with her? And what was that smirk for? She was clearly enjoying his discomfort, especially after his daughter had outdone her son in the class exams. And why did Gopal da need to be so fancy, insisting on a wedding in town? He was all for show, that man. And Amma, had she not lived enough of her life already, to indulge in such buffoonery in her old age. What business did she have riding off on a stranger's scooter? She had transformed into an attention seeker ever since that visit from her cousin, Jagat Bubu.

His chain of thought snapped as they reached Karmi village. Mohan jumped out of the jeep and ran towards the house of the scooter owner. The rest waited and, already convinced that he would return with Amma, drifted back into wedding talk—the money spent on decorations, the bride's finery, the way Amma had made everyone laugh with her relentless dance moves. Laxman prickled at the faint disparagement that laced their talk and was already reframing the reprimand he would deliver when he saw her.

Mohan returned without Amma. The scooter was rusted, unused for a year. Voices rose, questions overlapped, confusion ensued. Finally, a sharp raised voice suggested that they drive straight to the nearest police chowki to file a missing person complaint. It was risky to wait any longer.

As the jeep bumped down the hilly track, lit sporadically by tired pools of light from beaten-down lamp posts, Laxman was seized by a sense of doom, and his worry softened his feelings towards Amma. Who knew what had transpired behind closed doors after Jagat Bubu's visit, but a cantankerous Amma had transformed almost overnight into the most loved person in the village. It was Laxman who had urged Bubu, who lived in Bombay with his son, to come. He and Amma had grown up together, and she was especially fond of him. Everyone knew that after the death of her husband, Amma's fun-loving nature had changed, making her irascible and unpredictable. She had fought with her sister and son before landing on Laxman's doorstep.

'Where's my room?' she had demanded and looking at a surprised Rekha standing deferentially, yelled, 'Why do you stare like a monkey? Don't you serve tea when people come in from a long journey?'

Rekha had scurried into the kitchen while the children watched her from behind a curtain. Long-whispered discussions ensued behind closed doors, but Laxman decided that she was his nani and he could not turn her away. Soon, however, the family paid the price. Amma would hold onto grudges like a miser to his penny. Villagers began to avoid their house. A casual remark was enough to earn a lifelong enemy. She threw stones at the neighbour's children; before long Laxman's own children had no one to play with. Sales in his shop dried up. Everything slid downhill.

Until Jagat Bubu's visit.

After that, Amma was a different person. She often hung around at Laxman's dhaba regaling the men with jokes and songs, making it the village adda. Even Suresh, who ran the chai shop half a kilometre away, spent his days playing cards at Laxman's joint. His children clung to Amma for stories every night. Women gathered in the evenings to pour out their troubles, feeling lighter when they left. Amma still did no household work, but Laxman's wife no longer complained.

There was an excessive side to her friendliness, and her rambunctious jokes had caused Laxman embarrassment often enough. But now the thought of her lying in a pool of blood, her earrings torn away, or her body mauled somewhere in the forest, seized him so violently that he began murmuring a mantra to Hanuman, the finder of lost things. One by one the others joined in, their prayer rising and falling with the bumps on the road.

After three hours of an excruciatingly rough jeep ride, they finally reached Kapkot where the nearest police chowki was located. In this time, Laxman had composed several obituaries for Amma and an even larger number of reprimands for several people.

He leapt out of the jeep and rushed into the chowki. Seeing the hawaldar-in-charge fast asleep, he shook him hard, and inflicted on him a torrent of angry, incoherent blabbering.

The flummoxed hawaldar took a few moments to register what was going on. Then, bristling at Laxman's tone, he turned to the villagers who had crowded into the room and began firing questions.

Was the old woman completely sane?

After a brief discussion, which outraged Laxman, everyone agreed that she was.

Was she having an affair with anyone?

This was denied immediately, though Laxman was beside himself with rage. Did the hawaldar not have a grandmother of his own to ask such a question? Several people tugged at Laxman's sleeve, urging him to calm down.

Was she wearing a lot of jewellery?

At this Laxman jumped up and declared that Amma had been wearing at least five tolas of gold. She was attending a wedding after all.

The hawaldar paused, tapping his pen on the desk. Then, as though the idea has just occurred to him, he began to speak in cautious platitudes about theft and robberies.

Laxman lost all control. He launched into a tirade about a police force that could not protect its citizens, especially those from villages, whose lives were clearly of no consequence. The government, he thundered, had been promising a road to the village for years. Promises that vanished like vapour after every election. If there had been a proper road, none of this would have happened.

He was cut short by the hawaldar slamming his lathi on the table. He shouted at Laxman to shut up, demanding to know if he was drunk and whether he had given his grandmother the tonic too. It was purely a rhetorical question, and while Laxman began to splutter in outrage, the rest of the group fell into a sudden hush. After a moment's hesitation, Giri spoke up. It was not Laxman, he said, but Mohan who had been supplying Amma with drinks throughout the wedding.

Laxman spun around, staring wildly at the company, and let out a howl of disbelief. From the corner of his eye, he saw Mohan edging away and lunged at him. Grabbing him by the collar, he demanded to know why such rubbish was being spouted about his grandmother. Shame-faced, Mohan, whimpered that it was impossible to refuse Amma when she wanted something.

'Wanted what?' Laxman screamed.

'The booze, of course,' Mohan said.

'But why would she want it? Have you no shame?'

'But everyone in the village knows that she favours drinks,' Mohan replied, bewildered. 'What is so outrageous about it?'

Laxman began to rough him up. The villagers rushed in to separate them, mildly surprised at Laxman's sanctimony. Did he not know that Jagat Bubu had arranged for Indu's father, retired from the army, to supply Amma with a bottle from the canteen every week?

The hawaldar leaned back and shook his head, 'Doesn't know what's going on under his own roof, and he's here to educate the government.'

With the first rays of the sun, Amma woke up in the ditch she had fallen into when, on a sharp turn, she had rolled off the seat of the scooter. She had cried out to the driver, but he, drunk himself, did not realise she had fallen off and kept moving. Luckily this ditch was just off the road; otherwise, she would have rolled down the hillside. She was tired and horribly drunk, and the soft grass was so inviting that she fell into a deep sleep. At night, she heard a vehicle pass and thought she could hear voices calling out for her, but she told herself it was all a dream and promptly went back to sleep.

'Lord give me another day of fun, and I won't mind another night in the ditch,' she said looking up at the sky.

She climbed out of the ditch with little difficulty, brushed the grass and mud off her clothes and, now completely sober, if hungover, began walking towards the village. Soon a jeep came along, and she flagged it down, hitching a ride up to Khadkiya. Amma entertained the passengers with a raunchy song in lieu of a ticket.

> Under her ghaghra, the world turns slow,
> men lose their wits when she's on the go.
> Under her ghaghra empires are lost and born,
> be wary of her smile but more of her scorn.
> Under her ghaghra, mischief stays,

hidden like the sun in mountain haze,
elders cough and the young ones grin—
everyone knows, no one gives in.
She walks her road, she owes no man,
turns the village with her skirt's span,
and if you follow, don't complain—
it's your own heart you'll lose again.

At Khadkiya she received a grand reception and was treated to a bowl of hot Maggi noodles. After that a band of villagers walked back with her to her home. Luckily, someone remembered to call the search party, who, led by a bewildered Laxman, were stopping at every village and making inquiries.

Hearing that she was safe, Laxman began fuming with rage again. Bloody hopeless drunk! So that had been the reason for her transformation. And this was what she had been using her husband's army pension for. He had thought she was saving it, maybe even planning to leave it for him, to be used for his children's education. Her husband, his grandfather, must have plied her with drinks when he was alive, and when that stopped, her moods had swung. That older generation was an uneducated, degenerate lot! He cursed with strong passion.

Thank god his wife and daughter were cultured and would never indulge in such shameless habits. Like an illicit affair, everyone had known of this except the immediate family. How could he have been so blind?

Giri was muttering something about the loan that Amma had promised him, wondering if that promise still stood good. Laxman let out a gasp and shook his head in disbelief. No wonder Giri was so concerned about her safety!

Laxman's anger did not subside on the way home. It cooled and settled into a steely resolve. Even his companions, worn down by a night of searching, felt it had gone too far. Something had to be done about Amma.

When Laxman reached home, Amma had eaten a hearty meal and was regaling a group of children with the story of her disappearance. Rekha did not have the gumption to scold her, though she felt deeply embarrassed that Amma should be telling children about her drunken exploits. She could hear her use the word 'talli' several times followed by a gleeful clapping of her hands. The children were laughing loudly. Rekha had suspected that Amma was drinking but, so preposterous was the thought, that she had hesitated to say anything to her husband.

Laxman shouted at the kids to go home, waving a stick at them to drive them away. He pulled Amma roughly into her room and locked the door from inside. Rekha was surprised to see that Amma did not protest. She went completely silent. When Laxman came out, he had the keys to Amma's cupboard, which he held up and shook in the air like a trophy. She would now have nowhere to hide her booze or the money to buy it. Amma was to remain locked in her room for the day as punishment for all the trouble she had caused them.

The men huddled in a corner in Suresh's shop, listless, playing cards, wagering small amounts of money. Chamu studied the card in his hand, more out of habit than with any real strategy behind it.

'Did you manage to get the loan from someone?' he asked Giri.

Giri shook his head despondently. 'Who'll give me a loan in this god-forsaken village? Amma was my one hope, but—' He held his earlobes and bit his tongue dramatically. 'I dare not go anywhere near her now.'

A collective breath was drawn. The game stalled, cards forgotten, as they shook their heads in consternation, each man turning over the nasty stories circulating about Amma.

'My wife would spend her evenings with Amma, come back lighter.' Mohan said, slapping a card down to restart the game. 'But now she stays put at home and is constantly nagging me about this or that.'

'The village has gone quiet,' Chamu said, stifling a yawn. 'Too quiet.'

They played in silence for a few turns.

'Weren't you the one who said Laxman should rein Amma in?' Giri asked without looking up.

'We all said many things.' Chamu gathered the cards and aligned their edges carefully. 'I thought he'd shout, make a scene and in two days things would return to the way they were. But it's been two *months* since the wedding ...' His voice trailed off as he began dealing the tattered cards again with meticulous precision.

After a moment he called out, 'Suresh, bring some tea.'

Laxman stared into the fire that crackled aimlessly in the choolah in his empty teashop. He was heating the kettle for the fourth time.

His daughter came in from school and sat in a corner, sulking.

'What has bitten you?' Laxman asked.

'There's no one to play with,' she said. 'They said they won't come near me because my grandmother throws stones at them.'

Laxman looked at the unbought pouches of oil he had taken out to throw away, which had gone rancid, and at the vegetables rotting in the basket. He saw Giri trying to pass by unnoticed and invited him in for a glass of tea. Giri hurried on, mumbling that he had already had some at Suresh's teashop. Laxman poured himself some tea and slammed the kettle lid shut. The fire was dying. He bent down and blew into the choolah, ash and smoke stinging his eyes.

Straightening up, he dug into his pocket and took out the keys to Amma's cupboard. He turned to his daughter and placed them in her hand.

'Take these to Amma,' he said.

She stared at him, disbelief giving way to delight, and then she was gone, running down the path to their home, shouting, 'Amma! The keys to your cupboard!'

Laxman did not follow. He started stacking wood next to the choolah, humming a song to himself. Tomorrow he would go to Bharadi and get fresh supplies.

Hishalu

The ripe mustard crop swayed gently in the evening breeze, bathed in the golden glow of the setting sun. On a muddy patch at the edge of the field, Pushkar sat on his haunches holding his head in his hands. The outpouring of wretched grief had exhausted itself into occasional gasps and erratic convulsions in his chest. A calm had just settled into him when a child's loud wail reached him. The well of tears threatened to spill over again.

His eldest daughter, Dimpy, was calling out to him, emerging from a stone-and-slate house behind the fields. Her three-year-old sister, Sushma, who wailed in her arms, was settled against Dimpy's hip, the child's weight pulling her twelve-year-old body into a tilt that belonged to grown women. Seeing her approach, Pushkar gave in, burying his face into his hands and letting grief consume him all over again.

Dimpy came and stood beside him. 'Babu, Sushma won't stop crying.'

Pushkar raised his head briefly and said between sobs, 'Bechari ... what else can she do? Her mother is gone.'

'She is hungry, Babu,' said Dimpy, shifting the child to her other hip. Dimpy's stomach growled loudly, reminding her that she herself had not had a proper meal since dinner at a neighbour's the previous evening.

Pushkar struggled to reply when Himani Devi, who lived two terraced fields above them, shouted out, calling them for dinner. Dimpy immediately perked up and called out to Misha, her six-year-old sister. Soon, the three sisters were making their way rapidly up the fields.

'Why don't you come over too, Pushkar?' Himani Devi called out again. 'How long will you go on in this manner?'

'I've lost my appetite ... lost everything.'

Sushma began to cry again, and Dimpy, who had paused to check if their father would follow, turned and hurried on towards a much-needed meal.

Pushkar remained on his haunches in the mud, watching the sun slip behind the snow clad mountains.

As the morning peeled away the last layer of dark blue from the sky, the cock crowed stridently and set astir the courtyards of the village homes. Only Dimpy's house was lifeless, an air of neglect about it. That sense of order that Durga had maintained so meticulously in her life had dissipated quickly with her death.

Pushkar lay in deep sleep, curled up like a worm. The buffalo in the cowshed bellowed loudly, waking him with a start. He sprang out of bed and his eyes still closed, his feet began searching for his slippers.

'Three half plates rice and one full chicken,' he cried out.

When he opened his eyes, it took a moment for him to remember his new reality, and, with relief, sank back into bed, stretching his arms lazily, burrowing his head into the pillow and inhaling a deep breath of rest. It was not long before a child's shrill cry rang through the house and at the sound of it Pushkar's face crumpled into a ball of grief.

'Durga, O Durga …', he sobbed into the pillow, his hand reaching out to touch the glass bangles that hung on a wooden stand, glittering in the morning sun.

In another room, the three sisters lay on a large mattress which was laid out on wooden floorboards. Sushma's loud wail had woken up Dimpy.

'Ija, Sushma is crying!' she called out sleepily.

Receiving no response, she was about to call out for her mother again when she opened her eyes and saw her mother's empty bed. She stared at it for a long moment, hesitating to get up because then the day would begin. However, as Sushma's bawling became more persistent, Dimpy soothed her, shook off Misha, who clung to her in her sleep, and hurried into the kitchen to heat milk.

As the weeks crept by, the weight of responsibility of her sisters had helped Dimpy in moving past the sorrow. A weariness settled into her instead as she took over the reins of the house—an unconscious decision born of necessity, understood not through deliberation but through a quiet yielding to the expectations around her. The neighbours' generosity, in the form of meals and occasional help with chores, was always laced with baleful commiserations and lamentations over the family's tragedy. Dimpy knew that they needed to move beyond that shadow of gloom.

Now she sat by the choolah, a cloth tied around her head like an oversized turban, putting together a meal as best she could. When her sisters clamoured for a taste of her cooking, she told them to call their father in.

Pushkar lay under a large walnut tree in an advanced stage of dishevelment. He was playing at being dead, his mouth hanging open, his arms flung wide and his body absolutely still. Misha and Sushma emerged from the house calling out to him. Sensing their approach, Pushkar turned over onto his stomach and buried his face in the grass.

'Babu, Dimpy didi is calling you in for lunch,' Misha said. She and Sushma stood near him, watching him with a kind of wary curiosity, still not quite familiar with this man who had been away for so much of their lives till their mother's death.

When he did not stir, they tried to rouse him—poking, shaking, shouting into his ear—but he did not respond. Finally, clutching his arm they attempted to pull him up. Pushkar gave in at last. He slowly opened his eyes, rose and went into the house with them.

'Well done, Dimpy! How long could we depend on the neighbours' charity?' Pushkar said, sitting on the mud floor with Misha and Sushma while Dimpy served them khichdi from a beaten cooker.

'Pass the salt,' he said as he began to demolish a large mound of khichdi, pouring ghee over it liberally, not noticing Sushma, who held up her plate waiting to be served. Dimpy lifted her onto her lap and began to feed her.

'Teacher told me my hair is infested with lice,' Misha said. 'I have to cut it.'

'Is that so? I'll do it for you. A teacher's word must never be ignored,' Pushkar pontificated. 'Your guru is second only to God.'

The children listened to him attentively as he went on extolling the virtues of teachers, while shovelling khichdi into his mouth.

Later that evening, Dimpy was hauling a bucket of water across the courtyard to the cowshed. She groaned with the effort and glanced towards her father, in the hope that he would notice and help, but he was busy inspecting Misha's tangled tresses, a pair of large rusted scissors in his hand.

Misha sat before him, her head bowed in complete submission. Pushkar lifted small sections of her hair and began snipping them off indiscriminately. Little Sushma sat close by, watching intently, occasionally attempting to supervise.

A loud clang of the bucket slipping from Dimpy's hands made all of them look up and *snip*—Pushkar had cut a clump of hair dangerously close to the scalp.

'Careful, Dimpy! You'll muck up the whole courtyard if you spill that water,' Pushkar admonished her harshly.

'The bucket is too heavy. Why don't you carry it to the cowshed?' Dimpy shot back, her pride injured.

'Can't you see I'm busy? How am I supposed to manage everything?' Pushkar said, turning back to the mess of a haircut in front of him.

Realising that the haircut was now beyond saving, he made a show of trimming some more, but dropped the scissors soon enough and let out a long sigh.

'Here, Dimpy, why don't you finish this? I can't concentrate on anything; this terrible sorrow inside me is all-consuming.'

He got up abruptly and moved to the parapet where he sat down with drooping shoulders and dangled his legs over the edge. Dimpy stood rooted to the spot for a while and then, setting the bucket down and wiping her hands on her dress, went across to Misha. Misha, for her part, watched her suspiciously through the tangled mess flopping over her face. Picking up the scissors, which were too large for her hands, Dimpy looked at the irretrievable haircut with alarm, fearing greatly Misha's wrath.

'You better be careful,' Misha hissed as Dimpy attempted to even out the length.

Sushma got up to inspect the results and spotted the patch that Pushkar had cut too close. 'Oh! Didi has made you ganja,' she cried out.

Misha touched her head and felt the bald patch with horror. Flying into a rage, she began hitting Dimpy with her fists. 'What have you done? Everyone will laugh at me!'

Dimpy tried to push her away. 'It was Babu who cut your hair so close. I was only trying to fix it.'

But Misha's anger knew no bounds. She kept punching Dimpy, who tried to dodge her blows, glancing helplessly at Pushkar for reprieve.

'Misha beta, stop hitting her, she's your didi. Anyone can make a mistake,' Pushkar finally spoke up.

Dimpy stared at him aghast. 'Babu, *you* know it wasn't me ...'

But no one was listening to her. Misha continued her tirade against her, and Pushkar had already turned away. He was staring at the valley despondently when he noticed two women making their way up the slope towards the house. They were dressed in city clothes. Pushkar leapt up to greet them, straightening his hair and clothes.

After catching their breath, the older of the two, Garima, sat down on the parapet while the younger, Parul, went towards the girls, her pretty face lighting up at the sight of them. Misha had run into the cowshed as they entered the courtyard, ashamed of her haircut, while the other two sprung to their feet to greet them, their hands folded clumsily. Pushkar hovered around obsequiously near Garima, who explained to him that they belonged to an NGO that was working in the local school.

'You are Dimpy's father, right? It was very unfortunate, the incident with your wife,' Garima said gently. Pushkar lowered his gaze, his face taking on a woeful expression.

'But you must send Dimpy to school,' she continued, looking at the girls who were talking excitedly with Parul.

'Madam, the younger ones are attending school, but Dimpy is needed at home. How can I manage everything by myself?' Pushkar said, a note of defensiveness creeping in.

'I understand that your situation is difficult, but she is very bright, much ahead of the rest of the students in her class.'

'Is that so?' Pushkar was instantly delighted. 'Yes, she has always been very clever, right from when she was born,' he said, even as he turned around to look at Dimpy with mild disbelief.

'Pushkar ji, she must return to school. We will try for a government scholarship for her when she reaches sixth standard. I had told her mother about it.'

Hearing the mention of his wife, a morose look crept back onto Pushkar's face. Garima got up to leave, patting his shoulder sympathetically.

'I suppose you will be staying in the village now?'

'These poor wretches have lost their mother, I will have to sacrifice my career for them.'

'Dimpy, I will see you in school tomorrow,' Garima called out.

Pushkar watched them walking down the hillside with the awkward gait of those unused to the mountains. 'She will be there, Madam! After all, the pen is mightier than the sword. What would our society be without education?'

The fields were alive with the chatter of women as they harvested the mustard crop. Only the fields around Dimpy's house were unattended to.

Pushkar emerged from the house and stretched himself. He watched the women work as he soaked in the sunshine. After a while, he began walking down a narrow dirt path towards the small marketplace below. Spotting a bush laden with hishalus, wild yellow berries, he picked one and savoured its juicy sweetness. Then he picked a handful and stuffed them into his mouth.

Still munching, he stepped into Laxman's teashop. A group of gamblers was huddled in a corner, men squatting on their haunches, playing silently and intently. Among them sat Amma, Laxman's grandmother, wagering big money and making the rest nervous. Around them, a tight ring of men watched every move with rapt attention. Pushkar slipped into the circle of onlookers.

'Pushkar, have you eaten today?' Amma asked, not taking her eyes off the cards.

'The children will eat at school, Amma, and as for me, I'm happy to fill my stomach with hishalus,' Pushkar replied, not taking his eyes off the game.

'Hishalu, ghigharu, kilmora, bedu … do these make for a meal?' Amma scoffed and called out to Laxman, 'Serve him some food.'

Laxman brought him a plate of rice and dal, which he accepted without enthusiasm.

'Pushkar da, what did you do in Nainital?' asked a voice suddenly. It was Satish, a young man in flashy urban clothes, lounging on a table nearby.

'Hotel management,' replied Pushkar in a clipped voice.

'Management or bairagiri?' Amma snorted in her typical blunt manner, flashing a sharp look at Pushkar. 'If you had stayed back and worked hard in your fields, you might have had a better life. But you are not cut out for that, are you?'

There were soft sniggers and muted comments about Pushkar as if he wasn't there at all. No one contradicted Amma, but piqued, Pushkar shot back in an annoyed tone, 'Amma, do you think it was an easy life in Nainital? Up at five in the morning and on my feet all day. No time to sit, no time to eat—order upon order, cleaning tables, washing dishes … I would only get to sleep well past midnight.'

'Are you going back?' Satish asked.

'No way!' Pushkar declared. 'Who will look after the children if I do?'

Amma let out a short laugh. 'It was his wife who drove him to work.' Saying this, she slapped her cards down and having won the round, scooped the pot of money with both hands. There was a collective gasp followed by disappointed grunts. Seeing one of the gamblers get up to take a call, Pushkar slipped into his place and began to play. This would normally have caused an altercation, but the men looked at each other and, as if in a silent sympathy for Pushkar's recent bereavement and taking note of Amma's nod of approval, let it pass.

One of the gamblers, a wrinkled old man, spoke in a trembling voice, 'Durga was a strong, hard-working woman. Too bad she was bitten by that snake in the fields.'

'If there had been a hospital nearby, she could have been saved,' Laxman added ruefully. 'She was a good woman.'

Pushkar let out a loud sigh as he threw a card down. 'She didn't even leave me a son, did she?'

'Your house is running because of your daughters,' Laxman mocked him.

'You are so right, dajyoo. A daughter is worth a thousand sons! My daughters are the light of my life,' Pushkar said without so much as a blink.

Just then Garima and Parul entered the teashop. They looked around and greeted everyone. As soon as Pushkar caught sight of them, he quickly rearranged his face into a morose expression and threw up his hands, the cards scattering to the ground. This was the opportunity for the original gambler to slip back into his place. Spotting an empty wooden bench near the gamblers, the women settled down and ordered tea.

The old man looked up from his cards for the first time. 'How is your programme at the school progressing?'

Garima replied with exaggerated enthusiasm. 'It's going very well. The children! It's hard to believe how clever they are.'

Parul flashed a pretty smile, nodding and agreeing readily; however, the men exchanged uneasy glances, catching the note of condescension.

'Our children are so clever that when the world forgets to feed itself, they'll remember—and feed the rest of you too,' said Amma.

The bite in her voice unsettled Garima, and she turned her attention to Pushkar. 'I'm glad Dimpy is back in school, but she looks very tired. She told us she gets up very early to finish chores before coming to school. If she has to do well, she needs the care of an adult.'

No one can mind their own business, can they? Pushkar thought prickling at her tone. But he bit back the sharp words that rose to his tongue and threw up his hands again, 'People have no idea of the storm raging inside me! Madam, my brain as well as my life have come to a full stop.'

Garima was startled by this outburst but said nothing. Not receiving the desired sympathy from her nor any response from the company, Pushkar continued with a show of earnestness. 'But you are so right, madam. I will let nothing come in the way of her education. I will work hard in the fields and do everything I can for my children.' He looked around the gathering for approval with moist eyes.

Amma had won another round. She slapped down the cards again and burst into song.

All the fields were cut and gathered,
mustard tied and stacked away,
one man yawned and watched his standing—
'Plenty of time,' he'd always say.

One by one, the rest of the company joined the folk song, their voices rising together in an energetic chorus.

Birds flew in and ate their fill,
cows chewed slow along the way,
he lay back and called it kindness...
did not move from where he lay.

Then one night his pot lay empty,
not a grain to boil or fry,
from the hedge the sparrows chattered—
'Lazy hands let harvest fly.'

There was general laughter, and Satish slapped Pushkar on his back. Laxman smirked and passed him a glass of tea.

Pushkar rose abruptly and walked out of the shop. 'No time for tea. The crop is waiting.'

Deep in the jungle Khushboo gathered wood. She chopped dry branches vigorously and stacked them into a large bundle. After tying the bundle tightly with a length of rope, she hauled it on her head and began moving down the slope with rapid strides. Her lean body moved with grace, at odds with her shabby clothes, worn thin with use.

As she passed Dimpy's house, she heard a melancholic song. She paused, looking for the source. All she could see at first was a puff of smoke rising from the fields. Moving closer, she saw Pushkar lying amidst the crop, a bidi in one hand and a sickle in the other, its blade moving in rhythm with the song.

She could also make out three small figures in the fields—the sisters struggling with the crop. While Dimpy and Misha chopped the mustard stalks, Sushma dragged a large bamboo doka behind her to gather them. Seeing her struggle to climb from one field to the next, Khushboo moved towards them and, taking the hand of the youngest, pulled her up.

'You've put this little one to task too, have you, Dimpy?' she asked, a note of concern in her voice.

'She insists on helping, Khushboo didi,' Dimpy replied, a chunni knotted at her waist, her hair threaded with yellow mustard flowers, wiping her brow with a grown-up air that had settled into her manner.

Khushboo smiled with affection. She turned her head to look again at Pushkar, who was still invisible in the crop, only the haze of bidi smoke and the melancholic notes betraying his exact location. As if feeling her gaze, the sickle stopped mid-air, and the song faltered a second before resuming. With a helpless sigh, Khushboo moved on while Dimpy and her sisters got on with their work.

The mustard had long been harvested, and Dimpy had rejoined school. The house, however, had not returned to order—hay drifted across the courtyard, the tiles were caked with mud and vessels lay unwashed in a corner. Pushkar had settled into an idle rhythm, the allowance that Dimpy's diligence had given him. She had no way, yet, to counter his growing indolence.

The villagers were concerned too, but apart from lending an occasional hand, they felt there was not much they could do. Amma would bring over treats for the children sometimes, and unknown to Pushkar, had suggested that the matter be brought up in the next Panchayat meeting.

As Dimpy milked the cow, she watched her father sitting on his haunches on the parapet with Laalu, a slightly older man. They spoke in low voices, smoking bidis and staring at the snowy mountains. Sushma was up early, now painting a goat's hoof with a crayon, while Misha slept. After putting the milk away in the kitchen, Dimpy came out to hang clothes to dry, close to where the men were sitting.

'Khushboo! That one who is running around here and there all the time? Skinny and tall, always in shabby clothes? Surely I can do better than that, Laalu da.' Pushkar sounded offended.

'Johar Singh is very poor, and that is the only reason he is offering his daughter's hand to you. It will be impossible for you to get any other bride,' Laalu said.

'No, no. The very thought of marriage is intolerable, Laalu da. My daughters have suffered enough,' Pushkar shot back.

'Khushboo manages the entire household; her brother merely loafs around. She is the one who drives him to work in the fields. If she comes here, your house will be transformed.'

Dimpy slowed at the clothesline, shaking out a shirt longer than necessary.

'I will not inflict the curse of a stepmother on my children,' Pushkar averred, self-righteously.

'Well, think about it,' Was Laalu's parting shot as he got up to go. 'Your children are very young, and they need a mother's care.'

'I'm here to look after their needs.' Pushkar dismissed him, taking a deep puff of his bidi.

Dimpy stood still for a long moment, watching Laalu walk away. Her friends often teased her about getting a stepmother, making it sound like an inevitable tragedy that would befall her and her siblings. They recounted tales of other children with stepmothers, narrating the many cruelties heaped upon them with relish.

A little later, still full of mixed feelings, Dimpy was getting her sisters ready for school. As she hurriedly plaited Misha's hair with a ribbon, the two younger girls were already clawing at each other. When Dimpy accidentally pulled at her plait too hard, Misha landed a punch on her. From the path below, Dimpy's friends were calling out to her, urging her to hurry. At her wit's end, she looked at her father, who was sitting at the window and watching reels on his phone, letting out an occasional guffaw. A flicker of resentment crossed Dimpy's face.

He caught her look and, in one smooth movement, pressed his fingers to his forehead.

'This headache is refusing to go away,' he said gravely.

After dropping Sushma at the Anganwadi, Dimpy and Misha rushed down the slope to school. They heard the school bell going off and broke into a run. Misha rushed in through the school gates and took her place in the line-up for morning assembly. Dimpy, however, had noticed Khushboo working in her courtyard as she raced up to school. She had stopped for a moment to watch her. She saw Khushboo coaxing her brother awake as he lay asleep on the parapet. But then a sharp voice called Dimpy in, and she too ran in to join in the morning prayers.

After the prayers, it was time for slogans, the chorus led by the older students.

'Who will protect Mother India?' the leaders shouted with gusto.

'We will! We will!' the children roared in unison.

After the assembly was over, the children sat down on the grass for a general knowledge session. Dimpy's thoughts drifted back towards Khushboo. There had been something reassuring about the sight of her—her quick, sure movements, the easy strength she carried. To Dimpy, that sense of capability felt like something to hold on to, and her mind hurried to shape a small, indistinct wish.

'Name one king of France,' Mahipal Sir's voice cut through her thoughts.

'Loois the 17th,' answered a boy, springing up enthusiastically, relieved that he knew the answer.

'What is the currency of Russia?' The next question rang out, accompanied by the sound of the teacher's cane tapping impatiently against his palm.

'Dollar!' cried out a voice from the back of the assembly.

Mahipal Sir moved swiftly towards it, the cane quivering in anticipation when he noticed a scruffy boy whispering to his friends around him. The cane found its landing, and the loud yelps that followed snapped the entire assembly to attention.

Soon the children were asked to read on their own, while the teachers lounged on chairs nearby. As usual, Dimpy found herself drifting off to sleep, the early mornings and endless chores taking their toll. She could faintly hear the two male teachers gossiping in low voices.

'Those NGO ladies will be back soon to waste the children's time. What is the use of these workshops? Teaching children about birds and trees, as if they don't already have enough classwork,' Mahipal Sir complained.

At the mention of the workshop, Dimpy stirred awake.

'That Parul madam, she is something else, isn't she? Very delicate … very beautiful,' Lalit Sir said, with a sheepish snigger.

Mahipal Sir laughed. 'You should slip in a proposal when she is here this time. However, she could be married or engaged; it's hard to tell with these city people.'

'No, she is not married,' Lalit Sir replied quickly.

'You have done all the research, have you?' Mahipal Sir teased. 'But it's true that she is very different from other city women,' he conceded.

Dimpy was listening keenly, when she spotted Khushboo passing by. She had a big bundle of hay balanced on her head and stopped to speak to one of the female teachers.

'Dimpy! Focus on your work. You are so distracted these days,' Lalit Sir barked.

Embarrassed, Dimpy dug her head into her book and pretended to concentrate on the sums before her.

Dimpy yawned as she rolled out mattresses on the floor. Misha had already plonked herself on one and was complaining about having to eat the same food every day. Sushma hovered nearby, whining and tugging at Dimpy, begging her to play. Pushkar lounged on his cot in the next room, absorbed in his phone.

'Play with her for a while; she's only a child,' he called out.

'Why don't you give her your phone? She will be entertained for some time,' Dimpy snapped back.

Pushkar looked up, startled by her tone, but before he could respond, Misha chimed in. 'She'll sleep faster if you play with her. Otherwise she will keep whining for a long time and not let me sleep.'

Dimpy lay down on the mattress and drawing Sushma onto her knees began to rock her back and forth.

'Ghughuti, basuti, amm kaan cho ...' she sang in a sing-song voice, and Sushma squealed with delight.

Misha promptly sat up, demanding a turn. She pulled Sushma down and tried to clamber onto Dimpy's knees. Dimpy pushed her away, switched off the lights and lay down in bed.

A grumpy Misha called out to Pushkar, 'Babu, Sunita told me that Lalit Sir scolded Dimpy in class today.'

Dimpy knocked her lightly on the head and a tussle broke out.

'Were you being naughty in school, Dimpy? Beta, you must always obey your teachers. Teachers are only next to God ...' Pushkar droned, distracted.

'It was nothing. They were gossiping ...'

'What were they gossiping about?'

Dimpy did not reply immediately. The wind outside had pushed the door open. She got up to bolt it, her mind hurrying to form a scenario. She knew her father gave great weight to a teacher's word.

'What were they talking about?' Pushkar repeated impatiently.

'They were saying that she is very beautiful ... very different from everyone.'

'Who?' Pushkar had come to the doorway, his voice quivering with curiosity.

'Lalit Sir said he likes her very much.' A smile played on Dimpy's lips as she lay down again.

'Likes whom?'

'I don't know. But Khushboo was passing by at that time,' Dimpy said.

Pushkar came and sat on the ground next to her. 'Khushboo?! That Johar Singh's daughter?' He sounded incredulous.

'Yes.' Dimpy suppressed a laugh, struggling to keep an even tone to her voice.

'Really? Lalit Sir said that she is beautiful?'

'Hmmm.' Dimpy closed her eyes, pretending to drift into sleep.

Pushkar sat for a while, turning the thought over in his mind, *Khushboo? Beautiful?* Could Dimpy be mistaken? He returned to bed but lay awake still processing this new perspective on the village girl whose proposal he had dismissed so easily that very morning. At last, he muttered to himself, 'Yes, perhaps there is something in her.'

The next morning, Pushkar stood at the teashop buying rations when Khushboo passed by with the NGO women, carrying a crate of saplings. He greeted Garima and Parul, but his eyes lingered on Khushboo, watching her carefully for evidence of what had transpired the night before. She walked on, unaware of his scrutiny, her indifference stirring a new curiosity in him. He watched her until she disappeared around the bend.

The school was abuzz with activity. Garima and Parul were overseeing the planting of walnut and plum trees in every home. The children were divided into groups, and each group was accompanied by an adult from the village. Khushboo helped out with the distribution of the saplings and had pushed her brother to help out too, even though he hung back reluctantly. Each child picked up a sapling and marched off in groups in different directions. There was singing in the air and a lot of gleeful noise.

Dimpy's group had been assigned the task of planting saplings within the school premises under the supervision of Mahipal Sir and Lalit Sir.

'Your Parul madam is here. I say you take your chance as soon as possible,' Mahipal Sir said to Lalit Sir with a wink.

Dimpy's ears pricked up, and she slowed her pace so she could catch every word.

Lalit Sir sighed. 'I don't know if I can do it. What if she is offended?'

Mahipal Sir slapped him on his back playfully. 'You should have thought about that before you fell in love. Go on, I think you should propose marriage to her right away.'

Lalit Sir laughed nervously, moving ahead to join the group that Parul was supervising. Dimpy did not pay attention to any of it. Her mind was already racing, having found the fodder that she needed.

Dimpy sat next to the choolah making rotis while her sisters and Pushkar ate. Misha chattered excitedly about planting saplings in the village.

As Dimpy slapped another roti onto the tawa, she casually let out, 'Mahipal Sir and Lalit Sir supervised us today. They are gossiping all the time these days.'

Just as casually Pushkar asked, 'What were they gossiping about?'

Dimpy bent her head to hide a smile that had escaped her lips as she flipped the roti. 'Lalit sir said that he will propose marriage to her soon.'

Pushkar's hand froze midway to his mouth. 'To whom?'

Dimpy steadied her voice and pretended to concentrate on the roti baking over the fire. 'I don't know. But Khushboo was standing close by.'

Pushkar choked.

The roti had burnt, and Dimpy had to discard it, but one glance at Pushkar's expression told her that her work was done.

Pushkar lay on his bed. *A teacher from the city is planning to propose marriage to Khushboo?* He turned restlessly, feeling very indignant, as if something was being taken away from him. Somewhere in the churn of it a thought took hold of him. *Khushboo was his!* Soon he was calling out her name, an ecstasy rising within him.

In the adjoining room, a tired Dimpy finally lay down, a quiet anticipation churning in her stomach.

The next morning Pushkar stood before the mirror, combing his hair with unusual care. He had taken pains to dress well. *Not too bad looking, am I?* he thought, patting his face with a dab of fairness cream.

He waited for Laalu near the teashop. He held his breath as he saw Khushboo pass by, going into the shop to buy rations. He was suddenly shy as he watched her—her elegant gait, the swing of her long, thick plait against her back. He felt a hot rush of passion rising in him again. He reached out and plucked a wild flower from a roadside bush and filled his lungs with its aroma.

'Khushboo!' he whispered to himself as his object of desire passed by again with her bundle of rations.

When he saw Laalu approaching, he ran towards him, eager to speak out of everyone's earshot.

'Laalu da, you had mentioned Johar Singh's daughter that day …' He was suddenly nervous.

'Khushboo? Why, what about her?' Laalu refused to take the hint.

Pushkar blushed. 'I'm willing to marry her.'

Laalu looked at him curiously. 'I think there is another proposal they are considering for her …'

'But if she marries me, she will be close to her home,' Pushkar interjected with urgency. 'I can meet Johar Singh right away, and we can get married next week.'

Laalu blinked. 'That fast? What's the hurry?'

'Why wait? Johar Singh can make simple arrangements, and I don't want any dowry,' Pushkar declared with a note of self-righteousness.

'I don't think Johar has any dowry to give,' Laalu said dryly.

'I have to do this for my children,' Pushkar went on, swelling with purpose. 'So they can have a proper home, good food to eat. As for me … I can fill my stomach with hishalus.'

Khushboo's humble house was modestly decked out for the wedding. All the villagers had gathered to celebrate and partake of a simple feast. Dressed in her bridal clothes, Khushboo embraced her parents, preparing to leave.

Pushkar, the groom, looked very pleased with himself. The girls, dressed in new clothes, had not had so much fun in a long time. Dimpy ran around with her friends, laughing and shouting, something she had almost forgotten how to do.

Pushkar spotted Lalit Sir in the crowd and could not congratulate himself enough for having beaten him to it. He was surprised that Lalit Sir seemed to have taken the defeat rather well. Perhaps city people were more gracious in these situations, Pushkar thought to himself. In fact he appeared to have moved on quickly and was now very attentive to Parul, the NGO woman, who was also present.

The wedding procession began to leave the bride's house. Pushkar had arranged for a horse for himself which waited outside. He stepped forward and put his foot in the stirrup, when he heard Khushboo call out.

'Listen,' she said in a rather authoritative tone.

She was hauling a heavy suitcase—the sum total of her dowry.

Pushkar turned back and moved towards her shyly, not sure what she wanted of him. Khushboo came up to him and, without ceremony, handed over the heavy suitcase. He took it, taken aback, unable to protest. She already seemed in control of his life. A few men sniggered as he struggled with the weight. Pushkar glanced at the horse, wondering how he would manage both.

But Khushboo had already gathered the girls and one by one she lifted them onto the horse. Pushkar looked around confused, wanting to say something, but not sure what it was. However, the procession had already begun to move, the horse leading the way.

The sun shone brightly on the colourful assembly, on the musicians and the dancing villagers. The three sisters squealed with delight, perched high on the horse. Dimpy's body had relaxed into childish pleasure as she smiled down at Khushboo, who walked steadily beside them.

Behind them, Pushkar trudged uphill, brushing aside the beads of his bridal mukut, which swung from side to side, hauling the suitcase with difficulty. Most of the baraatis were too drunk to notice his plight or to offer any help. Amma and a group of ladies sang songs, walking just ahead of Pushkar.

Amma stopped to look at Pushkar. 'You just saved yourself from a dressing down by the panchayat.'

'What?' Pushkar strained to catch her words.

Amma laughed aloud. 'Blessings to you and your family, son,' she added kindly.

'I had to do it for the children,' he muttered, adjusting his grip on the suitcase. 'As for me, I can fill my stomach with hishalus.'

Acknowledgements

Written during the Covid lockdown, these stories came with a certain intensity and urgency, even as I stepped into fiction after several years of writing for film. The process, however, would not have been as fruitful without the friends who read and responded as I wrote.

My deepest gratitude to Billie (Aneel Bisht) for her tireless patience, invaluable feedback and unwavering generosity with her time. To Nisha Susan, for believing in my work and guiding it towards Westland. To Sanghamitra Biswas and Ajitha GS at Westland, for turning that faith into the book you now hold.

Kuntal, Gissy, Hansa, Molly and Subho—thank you for your attentive reading and thoughtful feedback. My son, Ruyak, for listening to these stories read aloud and, even at a young age, offering honest and perceptive responses.

To Paro and the many friends for their gentle nudges and encouragement, which kept me going.

And for the illustrations inside, Mrigank Negi